I0777901

LIOR APPELBOIM
D.E.U.S
CHILDREN
RECOMMENDED

WORKBOOK PRESS LLC
187 E Warm Springs Rd,
Suite B285 Las Vegas NV 89119 USA

Website: https://workbookpress.com/
Hotline: 1-888-818-4856
Email: admin@workbookpress.com

Ordering Information:

Quantity sales. Special discounts are available on quantity purchases by corporations, associations, and others. For details, contact the publisher at the address above.

Library of Congress Control Number:
ISBN-13:   978-1-965732-20-5   Paperback Version

REV. DATE: 02/13/2025

D.E.U.S

CHILDREN

LIOR APPELBOIM

CHAPTER 1

SHAUNA LEE- GUARDIAN OF DISEASE-

I, a young LDH- a lizard DEUS hybrid, woke up at my barracks and walked groggily to the cafeteria along with my peers, tail wagging with excitement. There I usually sit alone with only one person, my senior, serial number LH 619, Cobra, as everyone calls him. He has been the only friend I can speak with. He has been kind, sweet, supportive and never judgy. Even when I eat more than he does.

Today I ate three juicy green apples, washed them down with some nutrient water and ate a big bowl of fatty and nutritious porridge. He has always eaten less than me- half a cup of frozen berries and the army provisioned mush.

"Where are you deported this month?" I asked him as per usual, mouth filled with porridge.

"Today I've applied here," he said, chomping on frozen berries contentedly- "to help some on base operations."

"Then we'll have more time to catch up," I smiled cheerfully- "I should ask my supervisor to let us be alone after extraction, right?"

He perked up with glee. "Oh please do!" he answered excitedly- "we *really* need to catch up."

When we finished breakfast he stood up and stroked my hair- "send me a notice if we can be *alone* together, aight?"

I walked to my supervisor's office with a pep in my step and knocked gently on her door and when I heard affirmative then I skipped into her room.

"Has something good happened?" she asked with a twinkle in her eyes.

"Cobra asked to meet me alone after the extraction treatment," I answered cheerfully.

My supervisor sat up straight, grinning from ear to ear- "I'll see what I can do," she told me, sipping from her cup of dark coffee.

I thanked her profusely and gushed about how cool he was and how nice he was to me, that his stories were even more exciting the more we talked.

"I'll send him a notice," my super said- "since I trust you to believe that he's such a good match for you."

Then I walked around the room and did my usual tasks- doing basic warmups, taking care of my super's plants, making her some tea and leaving for my daily extraction appointment.

At the appointment we started as usual with a little smalltalk and a cup of relaxing tea. Then the extraction started. I put my mouth on a venom extractor and pushed my venom glands on it as hard as possible as the container filled up. I removed my fangs off the extractor and moved to the next one, then the next one and so on.

At the tenth one, I stopped producing enough for the whole container. The nurse slapped me across the face and cussed me out.

"You're useless!" "You have no worth!" "Why are you trying?!"

She hit me in the gut and smashed my face with a rubber club.

I was used to that.

I was already numb, the pain… turning hollow.

It seems there was no other way to extract more without life threats.

"Stop that!" Cobra's voice boomed. He aggressively held the attendant's hand keeping her from hitting me again. "Are you OK, Tails?" he asked me softly, taking the extractor off my face. "Let's go to your room," he told me with a warm smile, "I got approved to take you there."

I just weakly nodded and got up slowly. As I stood up I became horribly dizzy. He was there supporting me as we went out of the lab.

"Just what do you think you're doing?" the nurse asked.

Cobra turned around and smirked coyly. "I'll make sure she produces more."

"How then, Cobra?" the nurse demanded.

"A master doesn't share his secrets," he told them and took me to my room.

In my room he began unbuttoning his jacket, then shirt and took off his undershirt revealing his chiseled abs, tight chest and muscles.

He smirked confidently- "Like what you see?" Cobra asked as he began to walk towards me and placed his hands on my uniform- "I want to see all of you too." He looked at me hungrily, as if I were prey and he wanted to savor every bit of fear out of me.

He tried to unbutton my jacket but I jumped back- "We're going to have fun now," he said, breathing on my neck as if sniffing for my blood.

He then proceeded to take off my clothes slowly and gently kissing my neck and then taking off all his clothes and mine.

"You're… charming to look at," he said, pushing me to my bed- "I really want to… *know* you."

While we were--- pleasuring in my bed he continued to kiss me to muffle my cries, shoving his tongue down my throat and kissing my neck passionately. I felt comfort but also shame, disgust and glee. When we finished the venomous Cobra put his clothes on and left the room, leaving me barren and alone. After fifteen minutes he came back with venom extractor containers and gave them to me.

I put my fangs on each of the containers in turn and managed to squeeze out ten more containers of venom. He looked at each of them with pride, as if he had done all the work. "I'm gonna ask them to deploy me here," he said with greed- "I'm gonna show them I can do more than just fight."

He noticed my alarmed expression and looked at me, slowly smirking as if he were a hungry wolf focusing on his prey. "You're so adorable," he said holding my horrified face- "You look like a precious white hare." He caressed my scaly, freckled cheek- "And I'm going to help *you* produce more than ever before."

We continued this 'relationship' for three months, never saying anything to my super as he had told me. I was a good girl, as long as I didn't tell her I'd be safe. I hoped. I kept being Cobra's partner since he practically lived in my room, sleeping on my bed, eating with me, and protecting me from stares and gossip. At times he left our room for days, coming back only to smash and produce.

But he couldn't do it forever.

One day I went to the showers and tried to wash my shame away.

"Did you hear?" one of the female soldiers that I worked with said- "Cobra is planning on banging the venom cow from the coup three years ago."

"Why would he do *that*?" the friend asked- "She's become w-a-a-a-y timid and fatter since then."

What were they talking about?! I have no recollection of that or even being strong and confident, let alone staging a coup!

"Well," the first girl said, brushing it off, "I've no clue why she's changed so much-" She giggled- "I heard he's been moved here- 'cause of the fact that he banged one of his younger underlings."

The other girl gasped. "So he's doing the same thing to her?" she asked, "I still have no idea why."

"Tails is our venom cow correct?" Cobra's coworker said- "Maybe he found a way to increase her output through screwing her."

That does make a lot of sense.

Too much of it.

I continued to wash myself in defeat and silence. I guess this was all my worth to him, just a tool to pleasure himself and step back up the ranks again. The two girls left and noticed me on their way out glancing at me and giggling on their way out.

I finished my shower and got dressed. Then I looked at myself in the mirror and saw soulless eyes staring back at me. Why did I enjoy that?

Why am I afraid of doing that again? I'll finally be more useful and suffer less pain and recover from it, right? I do want more of that intoxicating pleasure, right?

I went back to my room without dinner. I didn't feel like eating, or doing my usual report to my super. In my room I didn't even want to read anything or even play any of my games. I took an extra futon out of my closet and turned the AC off in my room. It was winter, so slow time right now. I just planned on hibernating for as long as possible, maybe hopefully die in my sleep.

I don't know how much time had passed before I heard a knock on my locked door. "Tails?" my super called through the door- "Please, open your door!" she was alarmed- "are you OK?" She continued to pound on the door, and then I heard a rustle of keys.

The door clicked open and she rushed in. I didn't move from the coverless futon in my frozen room and as cold air streamed towards her she took her uniform off and covered me up.

"What are you doing?" she opened the ac on higher heat, then sat next to me rubbing me to bring heat back to my body- "I haven't heard from you in a week!"

I looked at her, bleary eyed. "I have no reason to stay around and be used until the end of my life-" I told her, heat activating my heart- "Either by violence-" I threw her off me and stood up- "Or by violation."

She looked horrified, and stood up and stared at the futon where I prayed to disappear. "I--I'm so sorry---" she whispered, tears welling in her eyes, "I-I knew what was happening in the usual extractions-" She looked straight at me with clear guilt in her eyes.

Then she locked the door behind us and did something on her notepad. "I'm not allowed to get my subordinates out of here-" She said, typing on her notepad aggressively, "but… the *least* I can do for you is to get you out of here," she threw her notepad on the floor, shattering it.

"But I can't be direct, as you're aware," she explained- "You need to do more of the legwork, and I have a friend outside who wanted to help you for years," she sighed in anguish- "but I declined because I was being watched, since I got that friend out before… So I was being 'punished' to be sent here and be a super to you, to make sure you were being kept complacent with the memory-suppressant drugs and turning a blind eye to your suffering."

"I always wanted to get you out of here-" She looked at the door determined as she told me her plan- "In two days the dead will be shipped out to the no-man's-land, you need to hide under the truck that is next to the cove. The moment you're in the biggest city of no-man's-land jump off immediately and run to any alleyway and wait in any of 'em for three more days for a Reacher to pick you up."

I stared at her. I'd always been a venom cow, right? Then, why, Why did she feel the need to be nice to me? Why was she feeling guilty for doing her job? It wasn't like she thought of me as more than a tool. Why?

I realized I needed to move forwards. I felt my confidence rising for a while after my super gave me a few energy pills to pop in my mouth so I wouldn't have to go anywhere completely hollow.

I went to the medical attendants locker room, opened my locker and looked inside it. As I was looking a nurse came by.

"What were you doing, Tails?" The nurse aske- "You haven't gone to a session for a week-" She scanned me from top to bottom- "Did you lose weight?"

"I have been exercising for a while," I lied through my fangs- "I thought that would increase my production." I smiled sheepishly.

"Well," the nurse said, sneering, "why don't we check?"

I agreed and went with her. I wanted to tell her that was a condition for my cooperation, but for my super's safety I needed to act like my usual timid self, even though I didn't feel like my 'usual' self.

An attendant came in with a cart of fifty containers looking confident as he set the first container. I filled them one after another until there was nothing left. No more containers, that is. The nurse and attendant just stared in shock and awe.

"This is the most she has produced in a week," the attendant said, looking at the aggravated nurse.

"It seems true," she hissed- "Fine-" She glared at her notepad, tapping on it aggressively, "I'll tell the higher-ups to put you back on power training and a change of diet."

I thanked her and went back to the lockers. I knew there was some stuff that I'd need there. I tapped the back which sounded hollow. I opened it and saw a big army bag with three bottles filled with two gallons of water, twenty-five packets of dried rations, a first aid kit with bandages, a small bag of painkillers, and ten adrenaline shots.

When I dug deeper I saw that my locker was connected to the morgue. I pushed the bag back in as forcibly as I could with my slightly stronger and scaley arm and closed the secret door and locked my locker and left for lunch.

A few hours ago my supervisor told me that my diet changes had been approved. I was given a big plate of scrambled eggs, a medium plate of well done beef and fried chicken breasts and a large cup of milky fruit smoothie.

During my lunch I could tell that people were staring at me, whispering. "Did ya hear?" murmured, "Cobra was sent away again," it was gossiped, "did he get caught again?" "Yes, he got caught banging multiple girls," gossip was buzzing around, "not just Tails? Huh…"

So the prick used me to jump the ranks in order to screw on other girls, welp sucks for him. I wonder what'll happen to him. hopefully more blocked promotions.

After dinner I headed to the morgue, hiding next to the boxes of the dead. It smelled horrible and I was looking for the opening where I hid my bag. I took it out of a small cubicle and jumped underneath the army truck. I swore someone saw me but they just led the attendants. A driver slid a notepad under the truck and walked away. I crawled to it and saw it wasn't very advanced and had no army seal on it. I took it as the truck began to roll away. The tremors of the wheels and the coughing purring of the engine kept me alert. We reached a blockade to check what's inside and if there're no runaways. They opened the back doors and a soldier picked under the truck and we locked eyes. He nodded but told his captain that it's all clear and we continued to no-man's-land. As we moved we came further and further from the ether lights as the sounds of the army turned muffled and dimmer.

Now the only sounds were of just the tremors of the wheels and the exhausted engine. I decided to climb on top of the truck from the blind spot of the drivers. I realized that I could climb like a gecko with both my arms and reached the top as a strong gust of freezing wind hit my face as I sat on top. I heaved heavily, exhausted from this minor workout.

After a while of time passed I saw patches of light all over. They looked like patches of stars, sparkly but dim. We reached a bustling small town market and my notepad beeped and blinked. I looked and saw a message from an unknown sender.

Time to get off, see ya soon. A friendly ally.

I took a deep breath and jumped off and rolled to the nearest alley. I rolled into a trash bin, fortunately I quickly sat up and caught it before I got smashed by it. After I straightened it up I sniffed a good sweet and savory scent. I opened the bin filled with "trash". I wouldn't call it trash there. There were salvageable parts for vehicles and computers, half filled bottles of fizzy juice that still smell great.

I saw a clean and dry box at the bottom of the trash. I picked it up and sniffed it. It smelled really good, sweet and savory, fatty too. I saw another box that smelled intoxicating and picked it up as well. I ate while walking around. The pink fish was strangely cooked, it was soft and juicy, it was better than any field cooked fish I've ever eaten, it tasted like flower nectar and of exotic seasoning. Not that I remember much. The 'pasta' was not overcooked and the sauce wasn't salty, but oddly flavourful. Why would people still discard edible food?

I sat down in front of a 'training' ground and watched. I was watching the kids 'train' and got a nostalgic feeling I really can't comprehend. Their 'training' wasn't training at all. Their game of Chase and Knock Out is just them tagging and immediately running away and shouting "you're it!". There were two girls rope jumping as two others rotated the rope at different speeds. Five other kids played with throwing a rock on chalk drawn from imprecise squares and rectangles at the shape of a strange ladder.

What's the point of this one though? I *may* get the chase game and rope, but the chalk ladder?

While I was deep into thought a large and coarse hand tapped on my shoulder. I flinched and jumped in fear from either getting hit again or getting hit on. When I looked up a man squatted in front of me and stretched his hand cautiously. He had sharp angelic-like features, dark, brown and messy hair, amber eyes that had a slit in them and they went immediately wide, as if looking at me for another reason that I couldn't figure out.

"Nice to finally see you out of there," he cocked his head to the side while looking puzzled as I felt, "you know me, right? Tails?"

"Not really, no…" I stared at him, confuzed.

"OH CRAP! RIGHT!" He turned around and showed me a photo of a boy with a beak on his face and hawk wings on it's back, "does that jog your memory?"

I stared at it and shook my head. "Doesn't ring a bell," I answered.

The man's shoulders slumped in defeat. He stood up and looked around, then he jumped on top of me and startled me, his face away from mine still looking back. "Phew…" he sighed in relief and stood back up, inching towards me in the process, "good thing I look much more human now--" the man stopped as he saw my horrified face, took a bit of distance and sat back down, "is everything okay, Tails?" he asked with odd concern, "did I do something awful?"

"N-n-no, you've done nothing wrong… so far," I mumbled, trying to keep my fear in check, he looked even more concerned, "s-s-sorry… I d-don't recognize you."

"Don't worry," the man said, he looked as if a light bulb sparked in his head, "I haven't introduced myself yet, huh?" he chuckled, "my name is Oliver Harper, my army nickname was Beaks."

Beaks, huh…? That does ring a small dim bell in the back of my mind. He might be a BH- a bird hybrid. He does have wings, they are just strategically hidden under his jacket.

"You can call me Ollie if you'd like," Harper stood up and stretched his rough hand to me, "you can take my hand or stand up by your own rules, I don't mind."

I was about to take his hand but decided to stand up on my own, with the heavy army bag on my back. Ollie smiled as he said, "I'm proud of you."

Oliver led me through snaking alleys until we reached a dead end backstreet. It was covered in graffiti of strange symbols like a feather looking rune and bird feet looking writings. He tapped the wall consecutively in order of one top one bottom two at the center three times. An eye opened and scanned Oliver, then he gestured to me to stand in front of the eye and it scanned me as well.

"Welcome home Shauna Lee, Oliver Harper," a machine voice welcomed us. I was looking around to see who this odd person named Shauna was.

"You're Shauna, silly," Oliver snickered as a door of light opened up from the wall, "let's go home," he welcomed me.

I followed him into the door and was enveloped in light. It was warm as we walked within the passageway. It seemed to be a portal that led us somewhere. I hoped I'd be safe wherever it led.

When we got to the end I was dazzled by a city-like facility filled with people, humans, D-kids and naturals old and young. After all, being a being of genetic engineering has no age.

I stepped back to swallow the entire city but was grabbed by Oliver. "Be careful," he said sternly, "you'll fall off." I looked behind me and stared down and saw we were incredibly high up in the sky.

"W-what? H-how?" I stumbled on my words, stumbling forwards bumping into Oliver. I could hear his heartbeat become faster and his face became flushed in red. "S-sorry," I apologized but he just cackled.

"I don't mind," he said, patting my head, "as long as you're okay, I'm good."

We walked off the edge into a town looking facility and on our way the people of the city were glancing at us, concerned. I was curious as to why they were worried. I looked at Ollie and he kept glaring at everyone, clearly uncomfortable and pissed.

A young wolf girl came running towards us, waving wildly and smiling wide. "Hey Ollie," she welcomed him, "haven't seen ya since three days ago," then she saw me, "and you are…?"

"Her name is Shauna," Oliver half heartedly introduced me to her, he held the bridge of his nose, annoyed beyond my expectation, "I'm gonna go to take my meds."

He began walking away as the girl shouted, "Call me when you need someone to drag you back to your room," she sighed in defeat as he walked further and further away, "he keeps dropping his problems onto a cup of rum."

"Why's that?" I asked, worried.

"I dunno," she slumped, annoyed and resigned, she looked over wherever he went off to, "he forgot about his report to Lila!" The she-wolf sighed.

"What is this place like Miss, umm…"

"It's Vulpa, Vulpa Wildwoolf" she chuckled awkwardly, "sorry for my half hearted introduction by the drunk Birdbrain."

"Nice to meet you Miss Wildwoolf," I said formally and she laughed wildly.

"There's no need for formality here," Vulpa explained, "here we're all equals," she took my arm, "our boss can tell you more about this place and better than any of us ever could."

We went towards a small building looking like a mayor's home with a big wooden door. Vulpa knocked on that door and it squeaked open and the both of us stepped inside. It was a single room house, with fabric and wooden furniture from couches to chairs and a warm fireplace with sizzling coals. On a big fabric chair, behind a wooden desk with a high tech computer and monitor stood a DC- a Dragon Cyborg unit- woman. She looked in her younger twenties, but the way she looked at Vulpa and I was warm and almost motherly. Her prosthetic eye shone as bright as the coal in her fireplace.

"We finally get to meet," She welcomed me with a friendly smile, "My name is Lila Smith," she shook my hand with both her metal and human hands, "Or also known as Angel, or as the first DC subject."

That would mean she's in her fifties by now, isn't she? She looks in her late twenties early thirties.

Angel saw my puzzled expression and giggled. "I don't look that old you think, hmm?" Lila asked me, "you're not the first to wonder that, trust me. I've wondered that myself to be honest," she snickered.

"I'm sorry I've distracted Ollie from giving his report," Vulpa bowed her head apologizing profusely, "he's taking his medication again and I couldn't stop him."

Angel patted Vulpa's head and shook her head. "It's not your fault," Lila comforted her, "he just doesn't want you to see him as a softie."

Vulpa looked up at me curiously. "What happened to give you the reason to leave the base you were at?" she asked with genuine concern."

I didn't want to.

I didn't want to.

I didn't want to.

My stomach wailed in pain. Burning with rage that was not my own. My throat tensed up and I began to vomit whatever was in my stomach, which was nothing but burning bile.

Everything went black.

OLIVER HARPER; CONSUMER OF MATTER-

My head is pounding but I haven't drank enough. Shot after shot and I still feel that Beast. The blackout of the destruction I caused not so long ago.

I'm at fault that it had awakened.

I'm at fault for many deaths of both enemies and allies.

I hate it.

I hate it.

I hate it.

Then I saw Tails' smile. The warmth of her voice and the kindness in her eyes. I wondered about my report and remembered that I hadn't done it and stumbled outside the bar, took a swig of my flask and wobbled quickly to Lila's office.

In her office I saw Shauna curled in a ball on Angel's lap and next to them was a pile of moving sludge. "What in the fucking hell happened here!?" I shouted and slid next to Lila and Shauna. Lila patted my pounding head.

"Nightmares," she answered, "that's how they controlled her."

I picked Shauna up while having a dizzy spell. "I'm gonna take her to her room," I blabbered in a drunken spell.

"Alright," she reluctantly agreed, "I'll be sending Russ over there."

The walk to her room was strenuous, people staring. They were whispering and judging. Why would they care for what I do? I'll drink as much as I need to forget. I just want everyone to mind their own business.

I hate everyone.

I hate everyone.

I hate everyone.

I stumbled up the stairs from the courtyard of the barracks then went up to her room putting her halfway down and supported her with one arm holding her hand around my shoulders and my other hand placed her hand on her door lock. The door opened and I dragged the both of us inside, tucked her into bed and went dozing off on her room's couch after taking one more sip of my meds.

I don't know how long I've been passed out when I was shaken awake by Vulpa shouting and shaking my shoulders wildly.

"I'm awake woolf, I'm awake," I mumbled.

"Russ is here," she flatly said, "he told me to get ya out of here."

I grumbled as I sat up, my head's pounding in pain.

Shauna was laying in bed with an IV and plugged into a heart rate monitor and hooked to a ventilator mask. Russ was next to her taking notes.

"Do I really have t--" Russell Catwalk glared at me and nodded, "you must," he nodded to Vulpa, "give him the hangover meds."

Vulpa took two small red pills and shoved them into my face. I swallowed them and coughed a bit. "Why the hell are you so aggressive?!" I raged but Vulpa shushed me and pointed at sleeping Tails.

I went out of Shauna's room and took a sip from my flask. I decided to go to Lila's lab, it's a high tech army-like shack behind her house-room-office-thing. I knocked on the door, after a few moments Angel opened the door and smiled a warm wide smile as she saw me.

"Are you okay Ollie?" she asked as she plugged an electrode into a jar with the pulsating Nightmare, "is anything weighing on your mind?"

"Nothing's going on," I lied through my teeth, my mind started sobering up.

"Please," she implored with concern, taking her eyes off the jar, "I want you to help me help you."

I sighed in defiance and tried to change the subject. "Are you going to purify this Nightmare?" I stared into the jar, "what was its purpose anyways?"

Lila sighed in defeat. "It's a smallfry that turns their host into a subdued and lazy sloth," she explained, connecting a few more tubes. "That's why Tails didn't want to leave at first."

"What triggered it though?" I wondered.

"The drugs they used to control the Nightmare and her will were wearing off," Lila thoroughly explained, "her will is stronger than the Nightmare's powers so her body's very will rejected it."

"What triggered it?" I asked Angel.

A knock was resounded through the small lab. "It's up to her to open up ya know," Lila told me opening the door, "hello there Shauna, welcome-welcome," Angel smiled leading her inside.

"Oliver…" Tails came towards me but my knees buckled and I began to cry, "I remember bits and pieces of what happened before--"

She stopped when I began to tap my pockets for my flask in order to stop my tears. Lila grabbed my flask with her tail and held it to her chest. "This is not a solution!" Lila yelled but I began to see red. I lounged at her, unaware of my emotions running wild again. Then I felt Shauna hug me from behind. I pushed her, grabbed my flask and went out.

I walked into our bar and filled my flask with whisky and asked the bartender for five shots of Spirytus Stawski. The bartender gave me one shot out of the five I asked for. "Why the hell would you not give me the five shots?" I asked while taking the shot.

"You have been cut off by Lady Lila," The snake bartender said, "you can fill the flask once a day as well," he looked at my flask and nodded, "this one is a freebie by the way."

I was enraged and threw the shot glass at him. "Fine then," I shouted and grumbled out. The other people outside the bar began to glare at me. I could feel them all judging me and hate whispering about me.

I felt a hand on my shoulder and turned around wildly, almost punching the person surprising me. It was Tails. "Do you wanna go to the garden for privacy?" she asked me with strain in her voice, as if she's afraid of me.

"Sure," I said, trying to look away, "if you're safe with me."

She looked at me, eyes wide in surprise and then awkwardly cheerful. "Thank you," Tails giggled.

When I'm with her I can feel stronger, more confident like those Nightmarish voices shut the hell up and I feel as if I could think for myself.

We reached the garden and sat under a tree overlooking a small bird fountain with the sound of flowing water and small bugs fluttering about. We tried to speak but cut each other off. Shauna giggled.

"Let's make a promise," she told me, holding her pinky for the offer, "I'll tell you what happened in the last three years, but you *must* do the same," Tails shoved her pinky in my face, "if you don't want to it's fine, but I'll won't trust you ever again and leave this place."

I was alarmed. "Where will you go?" I asked with intense worry.

"I dunno," she answered as a matter of fact, "Lila told me she'll help me get to the Earth sanctum, whatever it is."

"Fine," I held my pinky, "let's do this," we shook on the promise and a thunder sounded.

"W-what?" Shauna jumped, "o-oh… sounds like we made some kind of oath," she cackled, "it surprised me rather than terrified me."

"Understandable," I agreed and went quiet, nodding my head for her story.

After Tails calmed down she began to tell her story. I was horrified and felt grimly guilty, due to the fact that I know that I'm the very reason for her suffering. She was taken advantage of in so many ways that I couldn't look to her in the eye. The way she was okay for getting hit, violated by the guy she looked up to. It hurt for me as much as her voice quivered. Shauna told me that a few people helped her out and that's when she began to realize who she was and why she wanted to help me to recover from whatever pain I've been through.

I sighed in defeat and shared my story reluctantly.

For years the three of us had been used by the westerners' party, Tails, Fishsticks and I as collectors of many minor gods and the other-folk, Beast, Fish and Bird for experimentations by the bigwig scientists. Sometimes we'll have to kill the opposition, not asking questions we did.

"I may have looked like I was having fun," I said, "like I agreed with the killings. But seeing how you reacted as we went back to the base, I felt quite a lot of grief and a bit of moral tinge. That's why I orchestrated that coup, to make the higher ups understand our side.

"I lost my mind the moment I discovered there was a mole in our plan and we failed. When I woke up the entire base was razed to the ground. Fishsticks and Shauna were missing, I assumed you were gone forever and flew off drowning in pain and Landed at a nearby town.

"That's when Lila and her partner picked me up. They fed me, clothed me and gave me this shelter where many other refugees, humans and others like us. They gave me a job and a place to call my own, trying their best to help me trust others.

"But I couldn't even trust Lila or her partner. So I turned to alcohol to drown my pain, not reaching out to anyone and steaming in my guilt and loneliness.

"Until you caught up to me," I finished, "I would probably grab more drinks in secret."

"It wasn't the first time you were cut off?" Shauna asked.

"Not really," I answered in defeat, "I always force the bartenders for more," I smiled wryly, "this guy ain't the first one to apply there."

Shauna put her hand on my shoulder with a comforting smile. "We now can grow from our hells and improve ourselves," she then hugged me and I began to cry. I was about to grab my flask but stopped myself.

My thirst was strong but having my old friend trust me had changed a bit of my habits.

For now...

"Miss Lila did tell me," Shauna sat up, smiling reassuringly, "that our trio will be back together."

"You mean Fishsticks out?" I jumped up, "who's gonna reach him?"

She smiled wide, "us!"

DYLAN VANN; DIVIDER OF LANDS-

My codename's Gills. I'm an FH- a fish hybrid. While now I look more human, I used to look more fishy, like a combination of a duckling and a toad.

After I escaped the underwater facility where I and many more experiments were held. I sunk the place with my new allies. It sank all of the data gathered and landlubbers along with it.

The allies I've gathered began to sabotage many other underwater or coast bases for months each. We took rations and hindered machines, cut off lines etc. Every time we get an army's attention on us we move away.

We returned after a day of plunder and saw two strangers in our camp. I split the gang and went quietly back to the camp, using a new talent I mastered to hide in plain sight. The albino girl said with a familiar voice, "I doubt Gill would manage that large of an operation all on his own," she looked straight at me and smiled a snake-fang smile, "lone time no see partner."

I was startled and became visible immediately. "How could you tell?" I asked, resting my hand on my thigh knife, "who--" then I saw her wagging tail, partnered with the lack of front teeth, "Tails," I grabbed her behind me with my knife pulled out, "who's this guy?"

"Ohhh~ I'm hurt Fishsticks," the guy said, sarcastic, then chuckled, "I wouldn't recognise myself after my nice glow up."

"*B-Boss*," my closest buddy, Roger, whispered, "*what's going on?*"

Tails and Birdbrain shared a look. "We know where your members are hiding," Tails explained, "we didn't come for a fight."

I gestured for my guys to get out of cover. "Then," I inquired, "what for?"

"We came here for you, man," Beaks explained.

I tensed up and my guys grabbed their weapons. "We weren't sent by the army," Tails clarified, "aight?"

"Then who sent ya?" Roger stepped closer to Birdbrain claws out.

Beaks pulled out a notepad and I immediately grabbed it. When I was about to smash it Tails grabbed it out of my hand. "Elijah," she asked from the phone, "can you connect us to Miss Lila?"

"Understood," a warm digital voice and I saw it came from a human A.I. that looked oddly familiar.

Tails put her hand on my shoulder, moved me aside and stood at the center of our little party. A holo message was projected from the pad and a very familiar old ally showed herself. "Raptor…" I hissed.

She giggled. "Well, I haven't heard that nickname in years," Raptor snickered, "my official name is now--"

"DC-27," I snorted, "I know already!"

"No longer that," the cyborg explained, smiling sympathetically, "the names I go by are Lila Smith and the Cy-Watch hacker," she bowed in chivalry, "pleasure to meet you, head of the Sea Meister gang."

"You're the legendary Cy-Watch?!" Roger shoved in front of me, "Your work is the hardest I ever had the pleasure of hacking!"

"Boy I'm glad you're the one to hack my riddle-plagued code," she giggled like a teenage schoolgirl, "that one was made to train fledgelings for my industry."

"D-did I pass?" He asked, completely oblivious to my discomfort.

"That you did," she turned to me with concern, "will you come to my organization, Gills?"

Roger showed me his puppy-dog eyes and the others were looking at me to make my decision. "As long as we remain autonomous," I began, looking at the Cy-Watcher, "I'm willing to join you." I turned to the others and asked if there's any who wanted to stay to raise their hand. All hands remained down. "Now, Cy-Watcher," I turned back to her, "your side of the bargain."

She smiled affirmatively with a warm look in her eyes. "You can stay autonomous," Raptor smiled, "but I want to help you however I can."

"How can we trust you?" I asked but Roger tagged me on my shirt.

"She's been MIA for five years," he informed me, "she holds so much power over data that I bet she has others like us."

"I might help you reach places you couldn't before," Smith explained, "get you more recruits as well as further training for Roger to become the great hacker he can be."

"Why would you be so gracious?" I hissed, "do you have any ulterior motives to make us join y--"

"STOP THIS!" Tails looked at me, "if you don't want to come with us, fine- if you can't trust Lila, fine-" she begged me, "but why can't you trust me?"

The look she gave me, of desperation and… guilt? I averted my eyes. "You haven't changed at all Tails," I looked back at her, "always trusting--"

"I blamed myself for our recapture!" Tails began to chock up, "my trusting hurt me too many a time," she hugged herself tightly in frustration, "but going with Oliver to meet Miss Smith and her offer to let me reach for my old friend," Tails began to cry, "if I can help it," she looked up, tears running on her face, "I want to at least reconcile for my faults at our failure of a revolt," she fell to the ground, "I know you probably can't trust me after what I've done, or what've been done to us," Tails cried harder, "but please, we want to help you."

Birdbrain sat down next to her and patted her back, but she tensed up even more. "She had an awful experience before I reached out to her," he explained while getting up, "I had my own share of troubles, but Lila 'ain't one of em," he extended his hand to me, "we can tell you what happened to the both of us before we came to Lila's facility, and if you don't feel like staying out there and we will still assist you and your friends," I stared at his hand, Birdbrain looked at Raptor's hologram, asking for guidance.

"I will give you an ultimatum," The Raptor said looking at my burning untrusting eyes, "in three days from now you will have to make your choice," she told us firmly, "either you stay here and stagnante for the rest of your lives, or come under my wings, stay autonomous with all the benefits we offer you and help your team reach ever greater abilities than the ones you all have now."

"Why would you give me three days to decide?" I demanded.

"Because you still live as a soldier," Raptor answered straight up, "so you keep thinking the world is you against the enemy," she looked at Tails as she is still in shambles on the ground, "but you must be aware that your friends did not become your enemy."

I was surprised by her gentle voice and her guilty look when she gave Tails that were breaking down on the ground. "Would you mind if Tails stays here?" I asked without thinking.

Lila smiled. "Shauna," Raptor said warmly, waking her hologram next to her, "do you want to stay here with Gills for the three day ultimatum?"

Tai-- I meant Shauna, looked up at me and smiled weakly. "If I'm some kind of a trading chip," she said, "I'm used to that."

"Very well," Lila walked closer to her projector, "Ollie came back and Shauna stayed."

"B-but?!" Birdbrain tried to object.

"I'll be fine Oliver," Shauna sat up, "my mind's made up."

Oliver sighed in defeat, "just stay safe, 'aight?"

Tails just nodded weakly as Oliver picked up the phone and disappeared in a flash of light.

SHAUNA LEE; GUARDIAN OF DISEASE-

Dylan's guys prepared a sleeping bag for me right next to the fire and their boss's bed was right across where they placed mine. After I was set I got into the bag and dozed off in the heat and the comfort of being completely covered by the bag so no one could violate me while I'm asleep.

After a relatively peaceful sleep I woke up and it was quiet. I sat up and saw Dylan tending to the fire, then he got up and noticed I was awake.

"What would you like to eat?" he asked cautiously, "we have a bit of canned veggies, some preserved seafood and if you want I can go out and fish for fresh seafood but I dunno what I'll come up with so… we do also have some grains but I have no idea how to cook em."

"How about we make some seafood porridge?" I asked, "then everyone can eat even when it's cold."

He smirked. "On it."

Gills brought a big cauldron, a few canned vegetables, a few sacks of many types of grains, a few gallons of freshwater and a bucket of dried and preserved seafood. Then he gestured for me to start cooking but also signed for me that he'll jump for a few to find some fresh fish and jumped off the camp that was directly connected to the sea.

I put a bit more fuel to the fire, placed the cauldron carefully on the fire, put water inside and waited for it to boil, adding more fuel when needed. He came back with a small haul of different assortments of fish and shellfish when I started to put in the grains to cook. As he prepared the haul for cooking and preserving, he started to break the ice.

"How long has it been since you had cooking duty?" he asked, nostalgic.

"About five years and ten months give or take," I counted checking on the grain's state. It was softening so I added the dried and preserved seafood and waited a bit before adding the veggies.

"Wow… that long huh?" Dylan put the fresh seafood and fish into the cauldron, "thanks."

"What for?" I asked, apprehensive.

"For staying here," he answered, looking up at me but I averted my eyes, "what happened while you were captured?"

I felt uncomfortable. I didn't know how he'd react. He's my friend just like Ollie, but… I don't know why I'm scared. I don't know why I feel so unsafe.

"Take your time," Dylan told me, "I can tell you're troubled."

I should feel comforted, but I'm not. Why would he want me here? Why me and not Oliver? I thought they were closer than I was to either of them.

"Did Birdbrain do something to you?" he sounded pissed off, "if he did I'm gonna drown the bastard!"

I felt alarmed. More than I wanted to show.

"Let's finish cooking for now," he said while getting up with the leftovers of the gutted fish and prepared seafood, "we can talk about it while we eat."

We ate it in silence and The porridge was really good for what it was. Thanks to the dead air I decided to break the ice. "Oliver did nothing that hurt me," I explained, "it was someone else, at the base I was held at." Gills straightened up but kept his silence. "I-I-- got taken advantage of by a higher ranked soldier," I stumbled on my words taking into my mouth a few spoonfuls of porridge chewed quietly and swallowed through my tears, "I was used in… below the belt, forcefully."

Dylan placed his bowl on the ground, then he punched his hands on the ground as hard as he could, with a deafening crunch, fracturing his knuckles. He took a deep breath and I could tell he was holding back tears. "C-can I at least," he stumbled on his words, "know who the guy is so I can kill him?"

I was taken aback. "You aren't mad at me?" I blabbed out.

He looked confused. "Why would I be?"

I curled into a ball. "Because I let myself get used to it?"

Gills smirked. "Why would I be?" he repeated.

Dylan sat up and turned to his knuckles, staring with wide eyes at his fractured knuckles and sighed in resignation. I put my bowl down and crawled next to him and held his hands. "Are you okay next to me?" He asked with concern.

I shook my head but kept my energy focused on his knuckles. Saw the fractures and calmly spit on his hand my rejuvenating saliva to mend his fractured knuckles and looked up and locked eyes with him. I jumped back and crawled back to my bowl and we finished our food in silence.

"I still want to kill the bastard," Gills mumbled.

Then we heard the rest of his guys coming back after we finished our food and joyfully called to each other that there's fancy porridge for them to eat.

"Where did you send them?" I asked Dylan but this Roger guy looked at me with a spoonful in his maw.

"He sent us to look around to see where Cy-Watcher got her info---" He got cut off by another guy.

"The rest of us did a recon job in order to look for our next target," The cutter said, "Roger helped by hacking into many systems but failed others," the guy glared at him, "and we almost got caught, AGAIN!"

"If I had a better teacher I might've been able to change the cameras or turn the alarms off," Roger looked at Dylan with hopeful eyes.

"Why do you need me to decide for you?" Gills asked, "I may be the head here, but you have your own don't chu?"

"I-I know," Roger timidly answered, "but I don't want to hurt you…"

Dylan stared at him blankly.

"I-I know…" Hacker boy sighed and slumped back and sat next to the fire right next to me.

"Get away from her," Dylan hissed and Roger immediately skedaddled away from me, and from the fire.

I got up and sat next to the water and salt eroded window and stared at the sea, contemplating staying here. I was even more afraid of Gills than usual, which is saying a lot, since he tries to protect me by scaring others doesn't seem healthy.

He needs to come over to Lila's facility, but he can't trust her. I'm just afraid he had hurt his allies before, that's why they were scared out of their mind and pretty broken mentally.

"H-hey?" I heard Roger's timid voice from behind me, "a-are ya okay?"

I gestured to him to sit in front of me with an "I don't bite" look and he sat, and I continued to look at the sea.

"U-umm…" he looked around timidly, "how has it been at Cy-Watcher's facility? I'm incredibly curious…"

I smiled to myself. "After being born in the army you never get the novelty of this rare commodity of 'privacy'," I told him, "we all know that all too well, but at that facility you get your own room, your own stuff. You even get to go to higher education in stuff that you like or want to improve. Your group would probably get both its autonomy and help in getting info and as well further training or studies. You can even buy and sell commodities that your team can't or are unable to use. One man's trash is another's treasure, as the saying goes."

"That place sounds incredible," Roger sighed in awe, "I hope that you'll be able to reach him with that…"

"I will probably fail, or cause further harm to you--" I was cut off.

"I heard what this place is like to you," Dylan said, "but I'll have to fester on that for a while longer."

When we arrived at the outskirts of the facility Dylan and his gang keeled over and began vomiting violently. Each of them threw up strange, pulsating blobs of strange black matter. Five nurses came running with stretchers and picked the five new friends up and ran to the infirmary.

"D-did something like that come out of me?" I wearily asked.

Oliver went silent for a bit as he took his scanner from his pocket. As he put the scanner back in he looked at me with… guilt?

"Yeah," he confirmed, "however it was a few days before I got here."

"The time we initiated our revolt…" I pieced it up, "so… do all of them get their own rooms?"

"You should ask that knowledge from Lila," Ollie answered crudely.

"Then I'll go to her office," I began to walk away as he shouted from behind- "Can you at least help me pick those up?"

I turned around, peeved. "How?" I asked and saw him fighting those nightmarish blobs. Something within me burned, like the time of the coup. "Hold your breath!" I shouted and belched horrible gas from the bottom of my bowels as the blobs stopped moving.

Beaks pulled his wings out and flapped the gas out of the island. "When did you learn to do that?" Ollie wondered as he landed, "you weren't able to control that before."

I snickered. "I still don't," I answered, "it's more of an impulse rather than control."

"Huh…" Oliver responded, "can you help me grab those things," he poked the comatosed blobs, "while they're still out."

"Do we need a container for them?" I asked.

He chuckled. "You think I came unprepared?" Beaks asked, "fortunately for you," he grabbed his alcohol flask, "you were right," he took a swig out of it.

I was startled by his calm unpreparedness. "What?" Was all I could say.

I straightened myself and rolled up my sleeves and booked it into the plaza, looking for anyone that can give anything to contain those blobs.

Then I found one of the nurses and told him that we need to pick up a few blobs from the outskirts.

"Alright, alright," he said, "I have something that will purify those 'blobs'," he pulled out of his pocket a strange looking taser.

We went back and saw Oliver staring into nothing as the blobs started working up again. While the nurse ran to the blobs I walked to Beaks and slapped hard across his face. "Wha-what was that for?" Ollie asked in a dream-like state, he seemed to still be out of it.

"Wake up, idiot!" I shouted, but saw a blob latching into his shoulder and half his face, I turned to the nurse and the blobs only grew larger and larger as they merged together. "Wha-what's going on?!" I demanded.

"They're mutating!" The nurse explained, "what did ya do, Girly?"

"I spewed toxic gas out of myself," I brought the nurse to speed, "and they seemed to calm down though…"

"You… WHAT?" The nurse growled, "do you even know what those are?!"

"I-I don't!" I answered in desperation, "what are those things?!"

The nurse sighed and took his phone, and an ancient phone at that, and called someone on it. "Yes, we need ya right now," he told the recipient, "I'll keep Lila in her room--- I know that coming here will put everyone in danger! you're our last resort!-- Lila can't do anything when they're mutated and you can!-- Good, I'll contact her and keep a weakened sample to let Lila experiment on--- You know we have to so the other nurses can help when it happens next time, and if the Guardian of Disease is here, we'll need that!--"

He hung up the call then grabbed me and ran.

"Just tell me what those things are!" I demanded.

"No time right now!" He growled as he put a small vial of blob in his front pocket. I looked back as a Dragon Gate opened up and turned the blobs into… light? Photons? I dunno. Oliver was picked up by that light and the Gate closed behind him.

"What or who did that?!" I asked, unconsolable, "and what does it plan to do with Beaks?!"

Vulpa came running towards us as I began to pummel the nurse. She grabbed me and knocked me to the ground. "What happened here Russel?" She demanded, "where's Ollie?"

"He's been infected," the nurse stood up and dusted himself, "so I called the bigguns."

"How could he be so careless?!" She scowled.

"That's kinda my fault…" I apologized, "whatever I gassed on those nightmare blob things caused a fast mutation… according to the nurse."

"Is that true?" Vulpa let me go and I checked my wrists, Russel nodded.

"So you called *her* here to help him recover?" He nodded again.

"Just tell me what's going on here?" I continued, "and where in God's green earth was Oliver taken to?"

Vulpa glared at the grumbling cat nurse and looked back at me. "Oliver will be fine," she started, "the person on the other side is trustworthy," she glared at the point in the sky the Gate opened up, "she should've introduced herself on her own though," Vulpa looked at me and smiled, "those 'nightmare' blobs, as you rightfully called them, are actually lower power Nightmares," when Vulpa saw the puzzled look on my face she snickered, "I understand your confusion, I was on the same boat as you," she explained, "there's a difference between a nightmare when you sleep and those monstrosities that share the same name."

Vulpa and I began to walk back to the plaza as she began explaining that, Nightmares are beings that consume negativity in all of it's forms, from the Seven Deadly Sins to minor negative emotions like sadness or fear or even unconfidence. They can corrupt people in different potencies from pure rage and hatred or completely numb and complacent. They can manifest in many ways such as humanoids, animal-like and shapeless blobs as those we encountered today. Most Nightmares are indistinguishable messy blobs, they reproduce quickly and easy to control with certain drugs like the ones' the humans implant in their hybrid soldiers at birth. The more animalistic are less common and usually either work alongside humans or consume them at the flip of the hat. And the humanoids are the rarest and most eloquent, incredibly manipulative and unimaginably powerful. All of them thrive on negativity and preptuate more of it for their Mother, which no one ever saw.

"So this is a summary of what those blobs are," Vulpa concluded, "if you'd like to know more check on Lila or Russel," she was quiet for a moment, "but I'd recommend Lila then him, he's a nutcase and unpredictable so if you can't get Lila go to him," she grabbed my shoulders and locked eyes with me, "ONLY IF YOU MUST, OKAY?!"

I nodded violently, then she let go.

I *tried* to go to Lila's lab but was grabbed by the nurse that helped us before. "Russ, was it?" I wondered as he grumbled.

"It's Russell Catwalk," He grunted, "do call me Russ, but don't make a habit of it."

"Okay sir," I responded out of habit.

He took me to his lab and closed the door behind us. The place was incredibly messy and looked like it was a time rift, old machines alongside high tech research gear. Old but clean beds as well a lot of high maintenance materials.

"Welcome to my research lab, missy," he became much calmer. Somehow I felt less calm by that, "I really have to check the gas that you produced, and that mutation as well," he became jittery, hopping from one foot to the other scratching his arms, "then send my results to Lila for a solution and preventive measures."

He went around the lab and took a venom extractor and tried to give it to me but ended up shoving it into my face very violently.

I don't know what happened next because I whited out.

OLIVER HARPER; CONSUMER OF MATTER-

I was taken aback after Shauna decided to stay with Fishsticks for the last three days. Did she feel more comforted by him than me? I hope he'll not decide to come, I've lost too much already… I don't mind losing more, but not her. I feel like she was my lifeline, the thing that would hold me accountable for my drinking.

I've been drinking three days straight. I was so scared I would not be selected to pick Shauna back. I did recommend Vulpa to replace me in order to not see them, I was afraid Shauna would stay there if I came.

I felt a tap on my shoulder. It was firm and direct, like a clawed hand. "Why are you drinking now?" her voice said like sandpaper in my ears, "you have quite a few new friends to pick up!"

I looked at the she-wolf, groggy, dizzy and pissed off. "Why me?" I asked, "do I look okay enough to do that?"

"Lila told me to give this to you," she held her hand to my face and on it there was my sobering pill, "she decided that you are the only teacher she could send to reach out to them."

"Fishsticks hates me," I tried to take another swig of my vodka bottle, "and Shauna's scared of me," but Vulpa hit it out of my maw, "WHAT'S THAT FOR?!"

"What if they can only feel more comfortable with you?!" she screamed at me, "Shauna barely knows me let alone that Dylan guy!"

I looked at the pill with disgust. Getting sober is the last thing I want right now. The bartender slowly tried to take MY bottle of alcohol from me. As I tried to prevent them from taking my medicine Vulpa slapped me across my face. "WHAT'S WRONG WITH YOU?!" I shouted in rage, I saw her start to tear up.

"Why do you keep going to the bottom of the bottle when life's getting hard for you?" she pleaded, "everyone here cares about you just as much as anyone else!"

"That's my point," I glared at her, my head thumping, "I feel like I'm taking attention from the others… so the least I can do is treat myself with my medication while not bothering anyone," I chuckled, "maybe drop dead anytime soon."

She put the pill in my mouth and I swallowed it. "WHAT WAS THAT FOR?" I shouted, agitated.

"You're probably unaware that you hurt Lila when you drink," she dragged me out of the bar, "every sip you take doesn't just kill you inside, but also hurts those who care about you."

After a while of her dragging me to the nearest water vending machine, she grabbed a bottle and threw it at my face. I glared at her while opening the bottle and drank it with annoyance and silence.

"Have you sobered up?" Vulpa asked with her usual annoying tone.

I just continued to glare at her, finishing the water and squeezing the plastic. I got up and threw it in the nearest trash can and silently walked to Lila's office. "Not really," I said indifferently and walked away waving Vulpa the bird.

I haven't been sleeping properly during those three days. The days felt longer and more painful, just like the time I woke up in that back street after I morphed to a more humanoid look, just like Fishsticks.

I can't even trust myself around the guy. I feel at complete fault for their recapture and the more pain they've been through. I can only imagine what Dylan's been through to cause that morph in him.

He even learned new tricks after escaping, what the hell more can we offer him? He has a nice gig with his guys sabotaging and distracting all three nations at once and stealing their supplies. I saw the camp, they had enough rations to last a few years for the size of the gang. On the other hand they have a lot to offer us but Fishsticks can't trust us.

What if Shauna doesn't want to come back? I can handle Dylan not coming but not her. I'll feel even more hopeless if she's gone again.

I got over to Lila's office and knocked on the door, no answer. I decided to go to her lab since she'd probably be there since I'm usually uncomfortable at the office for some reason.

When I got to the lab Lila opened the door in a rush cursing under her breath and she bumped into me on her way out. She looked up and when she saw me she began to tear up, holding my shoulders tightly and looked directly into my eyes with worn out worry.

"I was so worried," she told me, "I didn't want to lose my family again!"

Lila pulled me into a hug and I was afraid to hug back. This is the first time I saw her so frail.

Then I decided to hug her back and she broke into tears. "I-I'm so sorry if I scared you," I confessed as she was completely torn apart.

"E-Eric's gone…" Lila cried while holding my chest, "I don't want to lose anyone ever again…"

I was caught off guard. Eric was like another big brother to me and he disappeared a few months ago and now getting the info of his death broke my heart just like hers. But I became listless, letting her cry while I just felt empty.

Lila calmed down and wiped her tears from her face and took a couple of deep breaths. She gestured to me to come inside her lab so I followed. The place was extremely cluttered but incredibly dust clean, wires and tools were thrown around but with method and purpose even if I couldn't tell what was which.

"Sorry about the mess…" she apologized profusely.

"As long as you can find a method in this madness I'm good," I insisted.

Angel smiled with comfort. "Thank you," she said, grateful. Then Lila started to tidy up a bit and a relatively new-looking gun fell out of her hands. I picked it up and was told to put it in the back drawer next to the purification setup over at the cleanest part of the lab. I decided to continue helping her clean, since I needed to clear my own mind as well.

When we finished cleaning up Lila thanked me profusely for my help but then she fell silent. "Are you 'aight?" I asked with worry.

"Will you go and check on Gills and Shauna?" She requested quietly of me, "I'll send Vulpa in your stead if you really feel upset."

I was slightly puzzled. "Were you waiting for my confirmation in order to send Vulpa," I wondered, "even when I recommended her in my stead?"

"I could tell you weren't in your right state of mind and waited for you to calm down," she clarified, "so I wanted Vulpa to make sure your answer was as sharp as you can possibly be."

"Give me the keys to the area's portal and I'll decide my answer when I'm ready, okay?" I answered and she chucked the keys at me.

"Do your best!" Lila yelled supportively as I was already heading out.

Dylan Vann; Divider of Lands-

I have my answer.

But I do have my gripes, since I don't know how much I can trust Raptor or even if I should. I worked with her once before on an apprehension mission in a no-man's-land city looking for a few deserters from the army. The time I was partnered with her was when I was ten years old, before I teamed up with Birdbrain and Tails.

The way she fought, and took many lives of innocent refugees and bystanders that were in our way. I am more afraid of Birdbrain and Tails for trusting her than anything.

I plan to get them out of her facility and find them safer places next to our camps. They may not want that, however. It sounds like the place is like heaven on earth, or wherever that is since I have never found it. But then again… my team and I always stay next to waterways so I can see why we couldn't even dream of such a place let alone make them leave such a place.

"Yo~" I heard a familiar annoying tone.

"Bir--" I was cut by Shauna.

"Oliver!" She ran to Beaks and hugged him in a chokehold. I used my powers to take the breath out of his lungs for a moment.

Oliver patted her head carefully. "Was it terrible with this sausage fest?" He cackled. Tails let go of the hug and dragged him towards the camp, "Will you tell us the answer?" Birdbrain asked with an indifferent face which annoyed me a bit.

I looked behind him, cautious of others and saw or sensed nothing. "You're alone?" I asked, still wary.

"I see your worry," he smirked, "but Angel told me that maybe it'll be more comforting for you if I'll be the one reaching out."

"Have you heard about our apprehension at Gladio town?" I inquired.

"Of course I had," Beaks nodded, "and I don't hold it against her."

"She picked you up like a stray from the street," I growled, "I'm not surprised you don't agree," I glared at his phone, "is she listening with this object right now?"

Beaks held his breath and smirked. I waited for an answer, Raptor probably wouldn't send one though… "I know what happened there," Oliver declared with grief, "she wasn't the one in control---"

"How can a soldier--" after I cut him the realization set in, "Oh, right… she's a cyborg."

"Yup," Birdbrain confirmed, "she feels enough guilt as is."

"I'll go," I whispered.

"B-boss…" my team stared at me with determined smiles all over.

Then Birdbrain grinned wide and Tails grabbed my hand giggling like a small child. "Let's go home!" She said and nodded to Beaks and he clicked a strange app and a Gate was opened next to us, "ladies first," Oliver chuckled and bowed deeply, "go ahead."

"You haven't changed a bit, ol' pal," I said and walked before the others as they snickered at Birdbrain's comment.

When the five of us stepped into the Gate a misty path lit up/ I was warm and cloudy like the sky during sunset. Tails ran in and grabbed my arm, then she began to drag us through the mist.

"Wh-what are you doin'?" I was startled.

"If we want everyone to arrive safely," she began to explain, "you need to know where you're going out here."

"And since you don't," Beaks came from behind us, "Shauna's your best guide other than myself."

"Then why aren't you at the lead?" Roger wondered and walked next to him.

"Someone needs to stay at the rear," Oliver explained, irritated, "so it's usually the one that opened it the last to leave this place."

"I see, I see," Roger then began pestering Birdbrain but I stopped listening to the two and focused on Shauna.

"So…" Shauna began, "what are you really planning when you meet Lila?"

I was a bit startled. "I haven't thought of that yet," I cautiously answered.

"You were so quiet while we were at the camp," she looked curious, "I just wondered what were you thinking about?"

I blushed. "I-I'm not going to answer that," I answered, flustered.

"Do you have a fever?" Tails asked and reached her hand to my forehead with worry.

"N-no, I-I'm fine," I took her soft hand off my forehead, "I-I was just planning on murdering the bastard that hurt you, is all…"

She snickered. "Are you gonna ask her about him?" Shauna mocked.

"Now there's an idea," I snickered.

Tails got quiet for a moment and poked in the air, then suddenly the end of the Gate opened up. "Roger, come over!" She shouted, "let Ollie stay a bit further so he can close the door behind us."

Roger discontently grumbled towards us. Tails smiled and pushed me through the Gate.

I began feeling a surge of pain from my gut. What happened next was unknown to me but everything went white.

OLIVER HARPER; CONSUMER OF MATTER-

I woke up on a soft bed and it was so soft as if it was made out of clouds, the pillow was extremely calming like there was a bubble of water inside it. I tried to sit up but I was pushed back as if I was weighed like ten times my bodyweight all over my limbs.

I moved my face to my right and saw a woman in her late twenties dressed in strange clothes, like a long jacket that was filled with more fabric, it looked incredibly heavy for someone to wear. Then I looked up and saw she had feathery ears. She turned her eyes and looked at me, when she noticed I woke up she smiled cheerfully and snapped her fingers.

The weight was gone and I immediately sat up and soaked in my surroundings. I was in an incredibly fancy and bright room, it was minimalistic with a closet, drawers next to my bed, a bookshelf filled to the brim with books, scrolls and tablets.

"W-where am I?" I spattered.

The woman giggled. "In my temple," she explained, "The Golden Dragon brought you here for recovery after your infection with a mutated Nightmare--"

"I was infected with a WHAT?" I tried to gather my thoughts, "how did that happen?"

"According to Her," she began explaining cryptically, "The Guardian of Disease has the ability to cause freak mutations in infections, such as viruses, bacteria and apparently Nightmares."

"She can cause that to humans too…" I mentioned, "so what happened next?! Is everyone on the island safe?!"

"Yes," she calmed me down, "The Golden Dragon purified them," she told me, "but you needed more care since you were actually directly infected by the mutation."

"I-I see," I took a deep breath, "but who are you?"

She stood up and twirled in the air and bowed. "I'm Ziz," she introduced herself cheerfully, "pleasure to meet you."

I slowly came to realize that I was in a temple of The very God of the sky and jolted out of the bed and was in the middle of confuzed saluting and bowing, not knowing what I should do to be respectful. Ziz giggled at my confusion. "You're my equal," she explained, "when it comes to the hierarchy of the divinity in this city."

I became confused. "What?"

Ziz giggled. "Do you think just anyone can come to my temple," she explained coldly, "have their own room in here and not stay in the public infirmary like everyone else?"

"Sorry for the disrespect," I sat back down on the bed, "but why me, your majesty…"

She giggled and glided towards me and kept floating inches from my face. "Don't bother respecting me," Ziz told me, "you are my equal in the hierarchy here."

"Wh-how?" I stuttered, flustered, "when…?"

Ziz sat next to me on the bed and put her hand on my cheek. "You don't remember me," she sounds sad, "don't ya, Sparrow?"

I stared at her blankly at the strange nickname. "Should I…?"

She laid on the bed, oddly crushed. "I used to be a human, ya know?" Ziz said, mostly to herself, "I met you after I was captured by the army," she raised her hand in front of her face, "due to this strange 'mutation' of this delusional purist," She sat up, "and became some sort of a God for the people here," Ziz looked at me with a desperate and exhausted smile, "I do need myself a friendly breath of fresh air, in between responsibilities."

I smiled awkwardly. "Even if we met back then," I began, "I might be more different than you remember…"

"I am aware of that, Oliver," she stood up and extended her hand to me, "but I'm going to help you be better than you were back then."

I took her hand and stood up. I turned back and saw the bed was dirty and messy. I was dirty and messy.

Ziz giggled when she saw the apologetic look on my face. "I'm taking you to clean yourself," she told me, "my attendants will help you," she nodded to an albino attendant, "while I go back to my responsibilities."

The moment the attendant approached me Ziz flew off to wherever her responsibilities were at the time.

The small attendant courteously guided me to a high class dust bath. While I stood by the door, completely puzzled, the servant walked ahead and bowed to me. "Is there a problem my lord?" He asked, still bowing, as if he was apologizing.

"I have no clue how to clean in this place…" I said awkwardly.

The servant looked confused. "I'm here to help you out, my lord," he explained, "that is my job after all."

I took off a bit of my clothes and then he stopped me when my wife beater and boxers were the last things to take off and guided me to the dust area itself. He told me to sit down and started plucking dirt out of my wings and I started a convo. "I'm a bit curious, why are most of the servants here are albino?"

"It is due to what our families consider our feather's colors as," he began to explain, "most families consider our white feathers as cursed and unfortunate, even if one with white feathers is born as eldest they are kicked out at birth or groomed to be a slave in different ways."

"There's harsh…" I agreed, "my friend is an albino lizard… I can't imagine her suffering if she was born like any of ya."

"You have a *lizard* friend?" He chuckled, but then hushed himself, "the beast folk have different rules than our own, I'll have you know."

"Let me just mention that we both were raised by humans to be tools of war…" I told him, "so our lot have no clue how to behave in your society or aware of normal society rules."

"I-I apologize for my presumptions, your highness," he told me, "I understand and will gladly teach."

When he finished cleaning me up we went outside and he dusted me with a feather brush and groomed my feathers with scented oil. Afterwards he brought the clothes and I saw them shimmer then realized that it had many layers, even folded up. "Can I have something simpler?" I asked, "I don't feel comfortable wearing something so luxurious…"

"You're going to have dinner with her majesty," He explained, "don't you think you should look your best?"

"She saw me at my worst, buddy," I explained, "I don't really give a damn about looking my best."

He just stared at me, then bowed and flew away and glided in with two layers of clothing, and after seeing the previous amount I agreed to wear these new clothes. They were a combination of wide and white parachute pants and a long golden robe tied with a belt and a red rope.

After we finished the servant guided me to the dining room and was startled by its size, it had many mirrors, windchimes, whirligigs and beautifully groomed plants. Near the table I barely recognize her majesty with a white t-shirt, blue pants and house slippers. "Ollie!" she waved and gestured to sit next to her, "is everything's aight?"

I was startled by her casual nature. But she felt more approachable now so I felt like I could take a bit of my walls down. "What's with the casual look?" I teased.

She giggled cheekily and poked me on my shoulder. I was startled, but it felt incredibly familiar. Then a name came to my mind, connecting to her face and personality. "E-Emile?" I cautiously mumbled and she stopped her playfulness, "th-that's the name that came to my mind… sorry if I'm off…"

Ziz got off her chair and hugged me crying. "I-it's my name!" she was blabbering, "it's amazing progress, Ollie!" she released me from her hug, cleared her throat and started piling food on my plate, "I really do need to update Ms. Smith about your progress…" Emile muttered to herself.

I perked up. "You have a safe contact with her?" I pleaded, "can I contact her right now?"

"It's very late in the day…" Emile awkwardly mentioned, "isn't she falling asleep about now?"

"I know that she rests," I began, "but not sleep like a normal person would… Like she updates Elijah's memory every evening and just rests after that."

Ziz seemed relieved. "Then we'll call her after dinner," she placed a bowl next to my filled to the brim plate, "eat up!"

There was duck breast with a sweet and tangy sauce, whole six hard boiled quail eggs marinated with veggies that are similar to eggplants, broccoli and radish, for grains I had some wheat looking white pearls with multicolored lentils and to top it all of there was chicken broth with noodles and veggies. Before I knew it my plate and bowl were empty. I tried to reach for seconds but Emile stopped me and shook her head.

She stood up and gestured me to follow her. Then when we left the room Ziz saw my confused face and snickered as we continued through the hallway. "Don't you think that the attendants deserve to eat too?" She smiled grievously.

"Sure," I answered, puzzled, "but what do you mean by that?"

"They only get the burnt leftovers of my worshipers' offerings," Emile explained, "that's why I share my perfect offerings with them."

"And you don't even deserve to be here!" A man's voice boomed from the end of the hallway, "you don't belong here."

"Tenku!" Emile cried, "don't disrespect my ol' friend!"

"I'll let your improper speech and clothes slide," he squacked, "but this guy is clearly not worthy of you! His aura is keeping its distance, and something else's clearly wrong with him!"

I began to glide away from Ziz and she shouted behind me. "Where are you going, Ollie?"

I glanced back at her coldly. "I clearly don't belong here, at the temple," I answered bitterly, "the guy clearly has more worth than me," I turned away, "he obviously has feelings for ya," I flew out of the entrance while Emile was shouting my name.

By the time I was far from the temple it became late, so I began to look around the oddly clean trash cans and found old rags and a few, very strong and half empty booze bottles. I sniffed the bottles and concluded the percentage of the alcohol was adequately high.

I flew off to an empty park nearby to drink myself to sleep. Sat on a bench and began drinking from the bottles until I blacked out.

The night turned to midnight and I flew to a quiet park, with not many folks around and the lamp lights are dim. The last bottle I took not long ago turned empty and I decided to conk out on a nearby bench and went out like a light.

Time passed and a bright light shone in my face. "Buddy," a voice called, "are you gonna ignore me?"

I turned away from the light. "I'm trying to…" I slit my eyes open, pissed off, but it seemed there was no one to glare at, "what?"

The light flew closer, taking some radiant humanoid shape. The more I stared at it the more I felt as if I'm looking in a mirror. "Finally you came to your senses bro," he said but I only kept staring, "still drunk?"

"Who--" I began to ask and he began to laugh.

"It might sound weird for ya," the mirror guy wiped his tears from this feat, "but I'm a manifestation of your good memories, if you will."

"How--" I was cut off again.

"You don't have the memory of creating me," he told me, "because you wanted to keep our positivity safe…"

"Protect 'us' from what?" I finally completed a sentence and his eyes went dim.

"From Malice," he explained, "the creature within us that drove me away," he smiled wryly, "your human self, turning to the Consumer of Matter," he started to glide to the center of the park where a giant statue of a majestic man with four wings, it was made out of copper but seemed to be ignored to oxidation, "we are the Creator of Matter," he stood next to me, looking up at the statue, "but in order to keep me safe, well… your good memories, you made me and sent me here in order to keep that nightmare from consuming me."

"That sounds like something that's impossible for me to do…"

"Well…" he smiled at me warmly, "you didn't know how to create me back then as well, ya know?"

"When did I create you?" I asked him.

He turned to me again. "That nightmare took form bit by bit when we went to the last war, seven years ago," he answered, "you probably remember our old allies dying left and right, the frustrations of failing to protect them---"

My heart sank to my stomach and only guilt built up.

"But--" He continued, "I remember that, at their funerals, we were treated kindly by their families," then his eyes dropped, "but at that was the moment I was born in order to protect every good interaction and memory you didn't want to lose…" he looked at me again, "but as a result, once that Nightmare took root within you, you began sending all of the good memories away, including Emile and every bit of our relationship… it kinda breaks my fabricated heart…"

"Can't you give me those memories back?" I asked, "I don't want to continue to wallow in my despair anymore, the guilt, the self hate…" I looked back up at the statue, the more I looked at it I saw myself as the person the statue was modeled after.

I went closer to it and the faded plaquett said the name that this memory mentioned - *Creator of Life*. But what does that mean? If I'm the same as this guy... Why did I have to be born this way? Wouldn't it've been better if I were born here, as a part of this world rather live amidst all wars and killing...?

"Lemme guess---" he flew next to me, "you hoped that you were born here, am I wrong?"

I was startled by him right in my face. "Well... you ain't wrong..."

"Well... bout that..." He chuckled, "the us right now was the only way for our previous form to keep the balance," he sat next to the palquard I was staring at and sighed flickering, "oh..." he looked at his hands, "time's up for me today," he looked at the sky breaking into dawn, "time for you to rest a bit, partner..." He snapped his fingers and I was out like a light.

I woke up to someone poking at my face, and I smacked their hand and opened my eyes. The sunlight was so bright I couldn't tell who woke me up. My head was pounding like mad.

"Thank God you're finally up!" a man's voice said in relief, "never saw a bird guy this awfully drunk before..."

I sat up, groggily piecing the shards of memory back together. Then I realized the trio that stood above me were humans. "How you lot ever managed to get all the way here...?" I asked while trying my best not to keel over the weight of my own head.

They looked at each other, trying to look calm and chill but failing in front of this drunk asshole. "What clan are ya-- you from?" the guy who woke me up asked formally. Too formally and I laughed, "are you okay bud--"

I began to lose it laughing and stopped due to a migraine.

"So-sorry 'bout that, bucko," I was given a water bottle by the girl that came with him, "no need to be so formal with me."

While I took a swig of the water the human guys sat next to me and awkwardly cackled. "Your clothes are quite fancy," he mentioned, "I'd assumed you're a member in this land's hierarchy, so I'd assumed you'd want this lowly human to give you the respect you deserve."

The way he said 'lowly human' sounded off and sarcastic.

"Are you human purists by chance?" I glared at them.

"Was it that obvious?" the guy that woke me up cackled, "I apologize for the di--"

I elbowed him in the gut. "You don't really apologize sincerely," I threw the bottle to the nearest trash can but missed, "if you chuckle like that."

The girl smirked at him.

"This guy's done with your crap," she snickered.

"Aren't ya in the same boat as that guy?" I asked, "You seem to associate yourself with this dunce, you're not much better…"

The third guy chuckled. "You meant that this guy is done with *our* crap, no?" the girl glared at him and tried to punch him mockingly but he still stopped her, "ya know I'm right, right?" They continued to wrangle.

My head began to pound again as the sun felt even brighter and the fighting friends. "I can go to a shaded area since you hate my very existence," I said, getting up as my legs buckled with every step and my wings being numb. I just keeled over and the guy that woke me got to me and supported my body.

"You prolly ain't gonna believe me now…" he took my arm over his shoulder and supported me, "but I don't hate your existence, ya know?"

The other guy came and supported my other side. "You seem to have alcohol poisoning, bud," he said, "how much did ya have to drink?"

"I dunno…" I was fading in and out consciousness as they carried me up to their apartment, closed the window and the girl ran to the kitchen and grabbed water and a heating pad in a kitchen towel and I was placed on my side and she gave me the bottle to hug. The rational guy went for a few seconds and covered me up with a weighted and heated blanket.

The guy that woke me up got out of the apartment to gods know where while the others made sure that I didn't lose consciousness. "Can you tell us your name?" The girl asked me as I felt like death was incoming.

"It's Oliver Harper…" I mumbled.

"Were you born like this or did your parents let you change?" She wondered and I felt myself heating up in anger.

"Do you really think I wanted to live this messy life?" I grumbled, "my ma was offered a high salary for them to carry me to term… so she took it, and loved me as her own… but I don't remember much myself…"

"How do ya mean?"

"Most of my positive memories are locked up somewhere else," I said with difficulty, "I don't know how I even manage to do that, but it's completely out of my brain or somethin'."

"Really…?" She was in awe, "then they might have not been all that posi--"

"Anna!" The rational guy that teased her before shouted from the kitchen, "can you check if Jordan's back, we're out of fresh ingredients for dinner."

"Dang!" She stood up and hurried to the window, jumping up and down fixed on the window, then ran to the button to open the window.

I heard the rustling of shopping bags and portable paramedic equipment being dragged and saw someone sitting next to me and taking my vitals. I tensed up as bad docs' memories came up. "You seem to be responsive," the person shone a PERRLA, a medical name for a very strong flashlight to check activity in the eye, at my face and began connecting me to a few monitors that started beeping. I stopped hearing people and was unconscious.

"Hey, bud," I heard that doppelganger voice but the room was warm and fuzzy, "you're at a crossroad right now."

"Meaning…?" I inquired.

"That you have your last choice," He explained, "let the negativity your Nightmare fosters with you and let it take control," his face became more and more clear, "or grab the pieces you gave me to guard, some of them carry the same emotions that your Nightmare amplified, thus they might become worse…" he extended his hand, smiling a crooked smile, "your call, partner…"

Then a monstrous beast huffed on my neck and I fell flat on my ass and looked up, horrified. The beast had my face but the familiarity ended with that. It had a body similar to a giant dinosaur, covered in dirty gold feathers, caked in muck and blood from the many wars we've been through over my life. Its claws were sharp and looked like they had freshly cut flesh, as meat and guts were stuck to them. The wings on its back were huge with sharp knife-like feathers that had quite a few missing, like the primaries were cut and the secondaries were torn, like a chicken in captivity.

"So, you've noticed, partner," the beast began to speak, its voice came from a mouth in its chest, it was… my voice! "You've done this to us!" He roared, "split us apart, never looking at us as your mighty ass just keeps on running ignoring our emotions!"

"But don't you desire to consume everything," The doppel asked the Nightmare with anger, "that's why I was kicked out to begin with!"

The beast laughed then cackled. "What choice did we have?!" It asked my doppel, "in war your only goal is the total destruction of one's enemy, is it not so? We sent you away so you'll not bother our partner!"

Hard to believe that a creature called the *Consumer of Matter* doesn't *want* to consume it to begin with… But all of us are a part of one consciousness, whether I like them or not…

I decided I'll take both of their burdens.

I will no longer run. I'll face both of them and find a way to reach those negative emotions my Nightmare fosters… And well those which are carried by the Image. I have to. Otherwise… everything Lila, Kuro, everyone in the rehab center, worked towards… Will be all for naught.

I faced the two quarreling beings and clapped my hands as a sound of thunder followed. "You both exist because of me," I began, "and my circumstances have changed, so I'll need ya both moving forwards," I glared at the Image and the beast and they turned their gazes from each other, stopping their fight.

"Are ya certain bud…?" The dopple asked, glancing at the beast, "that… *thing* will take everything you worked hard to protect--"

The beast chest maw disappeared and the creature was getting smaller and a smile came across the face, a peaceful smile. It was odd, seeing that monstrous creature smiling so gleefully like a child. It had a body that was incredibly similar to how I looked seven years ago.

"I do feel more positive now," The beast said in my younger voice, "thanks to our Judge."

Why does that sound oddly familiar? Oh well…

DYLAN VANN; DIVIDER OF LANDS-

My team and I got a tip from Lila about a sunken ship with materials and preserved supplies for the rehab and study organization she runs. I've never thought that the Raptor would be the one running this new home of lost folk, and for about fifteen years give or take. My only thoughts of her for years were due to the horrors she executed when I was seven years old. I still could hear the tortured screams of despair and pain from our already *captured* targets. But meeting Lila outside of the army, as the head of a self owned recovery program, I can see why people there will trust her with their lives.

She's kind, smart and resourceful, trustworthy, dependable and just. I see so many qualities that I haven't completely mastered on my own, and I want to be more autonomous than before she took us in.

When we reached the ship I split my gang to look for the supplies and the five of us headed inside from three entrances. two of my guys went into the hatch, another into the bridge then Roger and I got in through a hole in the haul. Roger was looking through boxes of waterworn machine parts while I was looking for rations, a little glowing fish swam in front of my eyes and twirled, as if asking me to follow it.

I decided to follow it and it led me to a health pod room, filled to the brim with whole, empty and broken but one. That pod was filled and semi-frozen, but I could tell something oddly powerful was inside. I wiped the glass cover and saw a girl, not even above the age of fifteen, looking frozen in time. I called Roger and he helped me to disconnect it from the wall.

"Never saw a survivor in such a condition," I said, lifting it with him, "or any other in those types of wrecks at all," I settled the pod on my shoulder and continued to carry it, "get what you can and head outside," I went on past him, "we need to inform Lila of our findings."

"B--boss?" Roger asked, "the girl looks dead--"

"Let me tell you," I held my position, "that even if she's dead, she still might be useful," I turned to glare at him.

"A-aight, sorry boss…" he apologized profusely, "I'll take as much as I can carry," Roger saluted, "meet you outside!" And he bolted off.

After a few minutes of waiting for Roger and the others I heard a voice, a girl's voice. "C-c-can y-you hear me?" She asked, the voice seemed to come from the pod. I looked at the pod and nodded. "U-u-umm…" she stuttered, "wh-who are you, sir?"

"My name is Dylan Vann, a fish hybrid," I introduced myself, "and what about ya, young Miss?"

"W-w-what year is it?" She skillfully avoided my question.

"It's the twentieth cycle since the Big War," I answered.

"I might've been here since a year before the war started," she told me, "I did know that it had ended since this ship had sunk, never realized how long I've been hibernating…"

"Hmm… I see," I agreed, "by the way, I have to ask," she went silent, "are you a fish hybrid?"

"Y-y-yes…" she confirmed, "w-w-why?"

"So I'll be able to release ya out here," I said and forcefully tried to open the pod. It then looked like she spread a bit of a frost she apparently could make to help me open the pod, and it opened at once.

She sat up in the open pod's maw and looked around, and then stared at me. My fellow mates came out of the ship and were surprised to see the girl that swam out of the pod and right behind me.

"Who's the pup?" one of the mates said and got smacked in the back of the head by another.

"Do ya have a name, minnow?" I asked her curiously and chummy.

"I-I d-d-don't have one," she whispered, "I d-d-don't remember my serial number, either…"

"How about we'll call ya…" A name came to mind, "Levia?"

She smiled cheerfully and hugged my back firmly, nodding into it.

"So, uhhh…" Roger began to ask, "what do we do with her?"

"Taking her to Lila of course," I said as a matter of fact, "do ye even need to sak?"

"U-u-umm, kinda…?" Roger mentioned, "you don't trust her much…"

I sighed while holding the bridge of my nose. "I truly can't deny that I don't fully trust her," I explained, "but she can get us bigger tips than just us going on recon," I look at Levia that held onto my back, "for example dear Levia was sealed here after all."

She looked at me with bright eyes. "Who's this Lila person?" she asked.

I smiled a wry smirk. "She's the one that sent us here," I explained.

"O-o-oh I-I-I see…" she mumbled, "that L-L-L-Lila gall must be a powerful goddess or somethin'…"

"She is incredible," I said, deep in thought, "but I don't know about her being a god or somethin'."

"I-I-I s-s-s-see…" Levia sounded disappointed.

Roger poked on the device that brought us to the area next to the ship and opened a portal while the others chucked the stuff they picked up and zipped back to the ship and got even more of the stuff they found.

"Do ya have a fear of height?" I asked Levia and she shook her head, I looked at the others and cradled her in my arms and swam through the portal and after a while of swimming we then fell through it and landed right besides the materials and the end of the main island cliff. I pretended to lose balance and she held onto my shirt until her knuckles went white, then I settled I burst out laughing when she bashed my chest.

I moved away from the edge and helped her to the ground and her feet buckled due to lost muscle strength, I helped her stand up and saw her for the fragile young girl she truly was. Levia was wearing a blue army issued two piece of short sleeves and shorts diving wetsuit and was pasty pale skin, her eyes were big green and bright aqua with large and deep, dilated black pupils. Her hair was straight, extremely long pitch- black hair, like the deepest and most dangerous of sea caves on the sides of the abyssal depth of the Mariana trench. Her tiny lips were blue due to both lack of sunlight and food, and it was filled with small knife sharp teeth.

After my guys came out of the sky hole one by one, Shauna and the she-wolf came running towards us and looked at our haul and cheerfully smiled as they looked through the stuff. While they were looking through the mess of rations and materials Lila came gliding towards us and the cold Levia tried to stand upright but kind of leaned on my chest instead, right in front of Ms. Lila, as if she had no apprehension of the fact that Lila is a cyborg.

"I'm glad Dylan's team found you," Lila bowed, "Lady Levia."

Levia was surprised by Lila's introduction. "I-I-I am Levia," she stuttered, "b-b-but I-I-I'm n-n-not who ya think I am…"

Lila laughed. "I believe you," she smiled brightly, "we need to check on you, healthwise that is," Lila took Levia's hand and saw my protective look, "I'm not taking her to Russ, in case you're worried," she sighed in defeat, and laughed quietly, "of course you can come with, she is definitely under your care, after all," Raptor looked at Levia with warmth in her eyes, "since you've both have been asleep for a while, after all."

SHAUNA LEE; GUARDIAN OF DISEASE-

When Lila took Dylan and the new girl, Levia, in the infirmary's direction as Russell scuttled after them but Lila told him off as it made he's head and ears slumped and he walked to a medbay stand by the market in the central plaza that was in the opposite direction to the indoor infirmary.

"Doesn't Lila trust Russ?" I wondered out loud, getting some strange materials from the sunken ship raid that Levia came with, "isn't he the head nurse here?"

"No one actually trusts that weasel," Vulpa answered my curiosity, putting ration tins inside a box she brought with us, "once he thinks a ship's sinking he's out of it and looks for the first research facility that'll accept his knowledge that he acquired in his years in other places."

"Really…?" I asked her back while sorting out the components and equipment that Dylan and his gang brought up, "didn't he save more than half of the folks' lives here?"

"He's a weasel first and foremost," Vulpa slammed a puffed up peas tin in the trash box, "he's a gas that fits itself to a container and behaves as the box commands and behaviors, and as people used say," she looked at me through the pile of materials and rations, "in rome- act like the romans."

"Do you believe we'll sink?" I asked, glaring at her.

"Naw, girl," she cackled, "but the weasel sure does hope for that so he'll have an excuse to leave all of the patients here."

From there on we separated the goods from the plunder in silence, while the merchants from the plaza came to pick up the filled boxes we had next to us, giving us small pouches filled with change and cash for the boxes they took.

"How long have I been doing this?" Vulpa asked herself.

"For as long as ya've been here," a brown skinned, slithery LH man in his twenties, "who's this cute chick that helps ya---?"

Vulpa punched him in the face. "She's not just a treat for your eyes, idiot!" she shouted, "you can't pick up every survivor girl just because they're cute?

He held his nose up as he bled. "Bitch," he said while glaring at her, "I was trying to be friendly to the new chick is all---"

"Do ya now?" She interrogated him, "what about yar ex, didn't she join us around eight years ago? Or the one that joined three months ago?" Vulpa smirked, "I can go on an' on, bucko?"

"Aight-aight-" he acknowledged in defeat, "some of my exes were new--"

"Then got dumped when a new chick came, hmm?" Vulpa cut him off with a conceited tone.

"Fine-fine, all of 'em?" He conceded, completely thrashed, "but I'm trying to be nice to the new girl is all, aight?"

Vulpa glared at him with doubt and skepticism, he flinched. "Do ya really wanna test my patience, buddy?"

I decided to leave this situation, as Vulpa acts in a terrifying and aggressive way that has scared everyone around us. I took a heating pad that I thought to use as a calming mechanism. When I began to leave the man continued to talk to Vulpa. "Why are ya goin' full mama-wolf all over me again?!" He asked, desperate, "is there-- GAH!" he was punched in the gut by her, gaining the attention of the customers and merchants of the plaza as they circled around those two.

"It's a question you don't wanna ask, buster," she told him cracking her knuckles, "and ya don't need an answer for that, capiche?!"

I shuffled out of the crowd and went to the infirmary to check on Dylan and Levia. The moment I left the scene I felt a bit guilty for leaving the guy with a raging Vulpa and a crowd of fifty stranger onlookers mocking him. I probably shouldn't feel as guilty as I do… but I still felt at fault.

I got to the indoor infirmary filled with nurses, hurt or sick people that are hybrids and quite a few humans, walking around, resting in beds while connected to I.V.s, some unconscious and connected to I.V.s and many monitors. I reached the farthermost and most secluded part of the infirmary where Dylan and Levia were seated. I looked around and noticed that Lila wasn't nearby. I thought she just was here to take care of Levia. Dylan looked in my direction then noticed me and beamed.

"How kind of you to check on us here?" he nodded to the girl, "go ahead and introduce yourself, doll."

"D-D-Dylan n-n-named me L-L-Levia," she introduced herself, teeth cluttering due to her weak and frozen seeming body, "wh-wh-what's y-your n-n-name, Miss…?"

"My name is Shauna Lee," I introduced myself cheerfully, "you look really freezing," I pulled the heating pad I found from the bag I was carrying, "would you like using this bottle to heat ya up?"

Dylan's eyes lit up. "Are ya sure you wanna give it?" he asked me cautiously, "won't you might need it sometime?"

I nodded and handed him the bottle and he went to the common area to fill it with boiling water, then returned with it covered with rags and handed it to Levia. The relief on her face when she fell asleep hugging it was worth giving the heating pad to her.

I quietly excused myself out of the curtained area but Dylan followed me and told me quietly that Lila asked for me to come to her main office, then closed the curtain behind him. I already planned to visit her, so I went out of the infirmary and went through the plaza that had quieted down quite a bit. The merchants were selling the stuff that many teams brought in and the customers were picking from the abundance that had been brought in. From preserved food rations to fresh fruits, vegetables and even many types of meat.

The smell from the street food stands was intoxicatingly good, many spices that are grown and dried by the residents here. I did decide to buy those octopus dumplings that are called 'takoyaki', the seller covered it up with shaved dried fish flakes, mayo and dried seaweeds that danced in the heat of the dumplings. I stabbed and ate it while I walked over to Lila's head office and finished them right outside it and threw the box in a trash can right next to the entrance then knocked on the door.

Lila's tail opened the door while she stood in the middle of a conversation with someone that sounded incredibly familiar.

"Oh, Shauna's here," Lila smiled cheerfully, and the man on the projector smiled warmly.

I stared for a few seconds until my memory clicked. "T-Terry?" I felt guilt building up inside, "where are you at?" I looked at Lila, "how did you manage to contact him?"

Terry laughed teasingly. "Apparently I went and became a God of Nature," his smile wavered, "are you okay, Tails?"

When he asked, I couldn't hold my heavy emotional breakdown. The guilt I felt for him was tearing me inside. I felt a big warm palm of hand laying on my shoulder, Terry's voice was extremely close. "You know you can tell me what's wrong… right?" His voice cracked as if he saw something awful, and I tried to muffle my cries. I didn't want to anger him with my tears. "Do you wanna see my garden at this time of day?"

I looked up, his eyes looked heartbroken, "maybe that'll cheer ya up, hmm?"

I silently nodded, wiping my tears, then he stood up and extended his hand to me. I took it and when I was up I let go of his hand and took a bit of distance from him. He went through the gate he made to come in and waited as I followed him and was embraced by the warmth of it.

After I came out of the gate Terry led me through, we arrived at his messy office. Paperwork was thrown on every slice of the tables in the room, some dust particles flew around with every breath and gentle steps.

"Sorry for the mess, Tails…" Terry apologized profusely, "I didn't think to clean this place for a while…" He chuckled awkwardly.

"It's completely fine, Terry," I haphazardly answered him, avoiding his gaze. My emotional strain was apparent to him and Terry extended his hand to me. I kept my hands to myself and he smiled gently when he came towards me.

"Can you tell me what's wrong?" He asked with care, "if you won't now," Terry kept his distance while smiling affirmatively, "then I'll wait until you do, okay?"

Terry sighed as he gestured for me to follow him and I did follow after him in silence. He opened an opaque greenhouse door and led me in.

The garden inside was gorgeous, rocks covered in glowing moss, multicolored fireflies lit the place up and shone the beauty of flowering vines, bushes and the colorful fruits on the trees. While swallowing the beauty of the little slice of heaven my first love had led me to, I noticed a few weak plants with sickly buds and scooted to them.

"This plant looks really sad…" I mentioned, cautiously picking at the wet ground, "am I seeing these wrong?"

"Well… you aren't wrong…" Terry admitted while he walked and scooted next to me, "it only responds to my true partner," he glanced at me and smiled reassuringly, "go ahead and touch it, okay?"

I was taken aback. "A-a-and what if it doesn't respond?" I asked, flummoxed and apprehensive, "what'll happen to me?"

He smiled and assured me that nothing bad will happen to me.

I took a deep breath and touched it. Life returned to its stems then leaves and bloomed the most beautiful blossom I've ever seen. Well, compared to the entire garden at least.

"I was right!" A woman's voice, "you wanted someone else!" The woman barged into the garden, "but I would've never expected a vile underdeveloped *reptile*!"

"The blossom proved her," Terry turned to her, "you have no voice here, Milla," Terry stood up and glared at her, telling her off coldly, I almost froze, "you and your family are not welcomed here unless for politics other than a union, understood?"

Milla huffed and walked off, slamming the greenhouse's door, cracking it. "Why did you mention 'union'?" I asked, anxious of his answer.

Terry went to the door and the crack and began mending it with a green glow. "We can take our time before we actually do anything, okay?" He answered me, then he finished to mend the door, "sorry for dumping this odd offer on you…"

I looked at the radiant blossom and my heart sank to my gut. "Do I even deserve you?" I mumbled. Terry heard but quietly led me out of the garden and took me to a room and gestured for me to head inside.

"I'm sorry to force this on you…" Terry apologized profusely, "but you're the only one I want to lead at my side," he smiled a wry smile, "take your time and care for yourself, aight?"

After he closed the door behind him, tears began to stream out of my eyes and I began to quietly bawl. A sharp pain sparked in my shoulder when I realized there was a knife stuck to my human shoulder. I looked around, sensing someone's cloth shuffle. "Who's there?" I demanded, "your aim was off if you planned to take me out," I snickered.

The would-be assassin got out of the shadows and the little thing was cloaked in a fuchsia pink and white fluff. Something about her didn't scream evil, more like order following type of malice, the type I'm all too familiar with. "Did Lady Milla send you to take me out?" I calmly continued, "then go ahead, make it quick."

She stepped back, startled. "You… you *want* me to take ya out?" The weasel asked, then her eye underneath glared with suspicion, "why?"

I went to sit on my new bed and gestured for her to sit next to me but she continued to stand. "We're in a similar boat here," I wiped my tears, "it may sound strange," I took a deep breath, smelling dried blood off of her, "but are you hurt?"

She almost jumped in her cloak. "Aren't you more worried about my knife in your back?" She glared, and I could tell that her fingers are bleeding badly.

I'll assume it's the reason she missed. Or that she wanted to play with me, her prey.

"I'll keep the knife until you either directly kill me," I bargained peacefully, "or we converse calmly," I smiled cheerfully, "I'll begin, I'm Shauna Lee, a western army deserter."

The weasel took off her hood and smiled. Her face was scared, one eye filled with cloudy liquid and the other was a vibrant ember but painfully bloodshot. Other than her out of place colorful clothes she looked like any common hybrid experiment I've seen before, more animalistic and misshapen but adorable as a button. "My name is Katerina," the weasel introduced herself, "as you can see, I'm pretty underdeveloped as a beast," Katerina looked around cautiously, "like you…"

I took in her words. "We're underdeveloped… is that what most of the hybrids are…?" I mumbled to myself.

Her eyes went wide. "What do you mean by that?" Katerina looked puzzled, "the Beast folk are no hybrids to begin with!" She shouted, insulted, but held her tongue, "but what do you mean by 'hybrids'?"

I sighed and told her of the world I came from, and how I came to know Behemoth, at the time the human Terry, who was a pure human and all but another experiment like me and many other folks on the outside. About the wars between the big three, the Eastern, the Northern and Western, where I'm from. Many soldiers are specifically bred and raised to give our lives during wars, and the fact that we're all replaceable.

She sheepishly came to sit next to me and listened with curiosity. "It isn't that much different than the politics here…" Katerina looked down on her colagulated bloodied fingers, "I was supposed to be the head of the Itachi clan," she began picking at the scabbed fingers and I put my hand on hers and prayed the damage away. "But due to me not passing the ceremony I was kicked out and my younger sister took my place…" A glow of ruby shone from my fingertips to hers as her eyes went wide again, "the pain…!" I took my hand off of hers, "th-thank you…!"

I stared at my hand with bewilderment. "I didn't know I could do that…" I took her knife out of my back, startling her. While I took it out I worked on the emotion that let me heal her and accelerated my cellular growth and pulled it cleanly out. "I guess like that…" I snickered to myself.

Katerina looked baffled. "You… didn't know?" She stared into my eyes with her one, "most of the reptile clans are healers you know?"

"I--" I began to explain but she hushed me and gave me a piece of paper and a nod, then zipped out of the room with a freezing breeze.

I looked at the piece of paper and it had a crudely drawn child's drawing of two weasel girls dubbed Katt and Sabrina, on the back was written a message with beautiful cursive letters, clearly the writing of an experienced, high-class adult. 'One day," it said, 'we'll be a family again. From your dear sister, Sabrina.'

The door opened as a terrified Terry ran into the room and sighed in relief when he saw me in one piece and hugged me tightly. "Y-y-you're choking me, Terry," I sputtered, then released me and he cupped my cheek and rubbed it as I began tearing up again. I took his hand off and apologized profusely, "I'm sorry… I'm so sorry…" I averted my gaze and continued to plead.

Terry sat next to me and sighed. "What for?" He inquired, "about your little assassin girl?" I clutched the drawing Katt gave me, Terry continued, "or is it about something you don't want to tell me…?"

I gasped, tears welling in my eyes, he smiled reassuringly. "I-I'm…" I began, "not pure enough for you…" I whispered, shaking, "I-I think I don't deserve you anymore… I'm afraid you'll hate me for that," I looked at his face and he smiled with… relief?

Terry warmly hugged me again and his breathing felt as if he was crying with me. "Such guilt…" He shakingly said, breathing painfully, then kissed my forehead, "you don't need to carry it anymore, aight Luv?" I looked into his eyes, painfully smiled and nodded quietly.

Oliver Harper; Consumer of Matter-

Beep…

Beep…

Beep…

I woke up to the sound of ringing in my ears and a flash of light shone to my face. "I'm up-I'm up--" I sat up and looked around, the Doc Bird sat up after checking my response, "lemme guess why you're here," I made a show of cluelessness, "did I get so drunk I became a social disturbance again?"

The Doc started to check my vitals quietly. "How much did you have to drink?" he finally asked.

I smirked cluelessly. "I have no clue!" I answered directly, "found a few half empty bottles and drank them," I finally realized I was in a lived in apartment that was incredibly messy, "how did I get here?"

"Do tell how many half bottles," the Doc continued, "and the alcohol percentage according to your estimate, if you will."

I stared blankly at him. "Why would ya ask that?" I inquired.

He just glared at me with disgust. "Your human allies told me you stank of alcohol when they picked you up," the Doc answered with venom in his breath, "so I'll ask again, how much did you have to drink?"

I chuckled. "About six or seven half bottles of some soju-smelling liquor," I pieced together from the broken memory that Image gave me, "so… I hope you can imagine how much alcohol I've had."

He became alarmed, shuffling paperwork and scribbled vitals intensely.

"You've had far too much alcohol," the Doc pulled a few herbal medicine pellets and mixed them in a water cup then gave it to me, "drink this."

I drank in full the bitter liquid that had tasted like clorox water with laundry detergent and gasped for air, my head clearing up from the intoxicating fog from waking up half witted. "You are aware this tastes awful, right?"

"It tastes awful because your body didn't want it," the Doc explained, "but you pushed through the disgust and finished the whole thing… how?" he whispered that question to himself.

"I'm an ex-soldier of the Western Unity," I answered his rhetorical question, "lemme say I've drank medicine that had tasted like burnt bio garbage," I chuckled, "so this mixture was actually cotton candy compared to this."

The Doc cackled. "Spoke like a true warrior," he nodded his head in reserved cheerfulness, "my name is Cohen, pleasure to be your acquaintance, my Lord."

I was startled. "Call me Ollie," I waved my hands in reassurance, "but why would you call me 'Lord'…?"

One of the humans, Jordan, was it? Came to the living room where they let me crash while being out like a light. "Lady Ziz gave us this letter after I brought Doc to take care of ya," he put on the coffee table in front of me, "she gave it to me personally when I was taking food from her offering box while I was looking for the doc," the man told me.

"And that was when I realized you must be some high noble," Cohen explained, then scratched the back of his neck, "but by your way of speech, you aren't *that* high ranking, now are you…?"

I blankly stared at the doc and then stumbled into a laughing fit, which startled everyone in the apartment. "I haven't laughed like that since Tails got her tail stuck in the base's vacuum cleaner," I wiped my laughing tears from my eyes, and sighed with a giant grin on my face, "how did I forget that?" I mumbled quietly, with a smile that hurt my cheeks.

"You okay there bud?" Jordan asked as he gave me another cup of water, "I heard from Anna that Your name is Oliver Harper, right?"

"Oh, yeah," I nodded, "I got two of you lots' names," I pointed at him, "you're Jordan…" and pointed at the woman, "and… you're Anna, right?"

They looked at each other with surprise. "You were badly poisoned," Anna mentioned, "how did ya get all that?"

"Being mostly a recon soldier has its advantages, I guess," I chuckled.

The third guy sat on another couch.

"You keep saying that you used to be a soldier," he mentioned, "then--"

"How did I get over here?" I finished his question, "I deserted the Western Unity base after I razed it to the ground--" I stopped myself, "and I don't like talking about it much…"

After that Cohen excused himself after he packed up his stuff as he bowed in goodbye and flew out.

"Shouldn't you go somewhere, bud?" The rational guy asked me.

"Your name," I blatantly said.

"What?" He asked.

"I know two peeps out of three," I explained, "your name, bud."

He laughed incredibly loud with tears coming out of his eyes. "Understood," he calmed down a bit, "it's Alexander, but you can call me Alex," Al chuckled, "I'll call ya Ollie if ya don't mind, bud."

"I don't mind," a cup of warm and sweet herbal tea was in my hand, I looked up and saw that Anna made some, "it ain't that medicine I was given before now is it?"

She giggled. "I made a pot for everyone, so no," Anna explained and held her own cup, Jordan leaving the kitchen with two more cups, "Cohen just left, J…" she mentioned.

"Oh, I know," Jordan came into the living room, placing a cup on a mantle with a printed picture surrounded by flowers and incense, "I just wanted to offer our friend his favorite tea…" He held his hands in prayer.

"Who are you talking about…?" I wondered between sips.

Anna sat next to me and sighed. "One of us that didn't successfully make it here…" She told me, "he was really sick, and he died during the questioning in order to find Emille-- I mean Ziz."

"You can call her that around me," I explained with a smile, "I knew her by that name to begin with--"

"Oh!" Alex looked out of the entrance window, opened it and smiled cockily, "look who decided to visit this humble abode."

A wing flap and a giggle came through the entrance and a familiar face came from across the wall. It was Emile in a more casual T-shirt and shorts. "Has Ollie been troubling you?" she asked Alex, "thank you lot for helping him out," Emile bowed her head in gratitude and hobbled cautiously to sit next to me.

I smiled affirmatively, put my hand on her side and hugged her as if I was a pup. She looked at me startled but then smiled from ear to ear and returned the hug. "What's going on…?" Jordan came to the living room, awkward, "I thought you hated her, bud…"

I laughed. "I never 'hated' her as much as I locked myself away," I explained, I looked at her with a smirk, "I kinda felt unworthy for your over familiarity with me," I told her, "now I remember why you were."

I pecked her forehead affectionately and smiled.

Emile looked like she was over the moon and grabbed my hand. "Let's go to the temple," she told me, Emile looked at Jordan as he smiled a sad smile and nodded, "thank you all for helping Ollie--"

"Even though we didn't do much?" Anna asked.

"You lot basically saved my life by bringing a doc to clear my stomach out," I looked at Jordan, "I don't think I've been able to make it if you haven't brought the guy," I looked at Anna, "the water you gave me was real helpful to sober me up," I got up with Emile, "I hope I wasn't *that* much of a hassle," I bowed in gratitude and flew out and Emile followed me out and giggling.

Dylan Vann; Divider of Lands-

After Lila cleared Levia to leave the infirmary, Levia jumped off her bed and dragged me out of it, practically glued to my arm. She kept looking around and dragging me along. We talked to merchants and occupants and the fact she has no new clothes for herself since she arrived here.

"I'll let you borrow a few of my spare clothes, doll," I told her, "I'll buy you new ones when I get paid, aight?"

She jumped cheerfully up and down. "You sure you don't mind, hun?"

After she said that we got a look from the old merchant lady. "What a lovely couple you two are," she smiled and gave her a big shawl.

"Thank you, ma'am…" I smiled and took Levia away to prevent myself from saying something stupid and make Levia lose her smile.

We went to a side park that was empty and overgrown but it's incredibly beautiful. That was where me and my guys camped out since we didn't want to officially be a part of this organization so this was the solution that Raptor came up with. Our sleeping bags and belonging filled boxes were placed around an old but working classical fountain for us to stay wet while we stay here.

I went to my box and dug through it. I pulled two nice T-shirts and my old but good condition bomber jacket in case she'll be freezing again.

My old journal fell out while I was putting everything back in my box, Levia noticed and tried to pick it up. "Sorry, doll," I told her after dropping my stuff and picked my journal in a rush, "no one is allowed to read it, not even my buddies know it even exists…"

She stared at me with her big curious eyes. "Then…" Levia declared cautiously, "what does that make me?"

I smiled after I got everything into the box. "A very unlucky friend, doll…" I answered with a dry smile.

"Why's that, Dylan?" She kept pestering me, "I think you're a great person, ya know?"

I slammed my hands on the fountain sides and sighed. "You know nothing---"

"Then how'll I know," she declared with worry, "if ya don't let me in?!"

"Then don't try…" I answered coldly.

I heard her begin to sob, then she ran out of the garden blubbering all the way. My heart ached, but I believe it'll be better for her to stay away from me. I don't deserve people's love, just their respect is enough for me. A lonely existence, but a deserving one.

I picked up my old journal and started skimming through it. It's filled with entries that were so methodical and cold, everything had a date and year, introduction and everything that happened each day. No emotion was shown there, no concern for peoples' lives, no awareness of loss and even guilt.

I believed that if anyone ever read it, they'd be disgusted at me and never want to be my friends. That's the reason why I didn't want Levia to even look at it… I don't want to lose her. Or anyone ever again.

Roger came running to my spot when I hid my journal back in my box. "Boss, Boss!" He came waving an envelope, "this is our paycheque for the last mission--" He looked around, "where's the new girl--" when he saw my hurt look, "did'ja scare her off again?" I glared at him, and he chuckled, "I'll guess," he went to sit next to me on the fountain, leaning into my face, "it's a yay from me dawg."

Something in his question puzzled me. "What do ya mean by 'again'?"

Roger stared blankly at me. "You okay, Boss…?" He asked, cocking his head to the side with bewilderment, "she was in the same facility as you an' I, don't chu remember?"

Was I familiar with her from before…? Was that's why I was so familiar with her subconsciously? Was that why I was this hurt by seeing her cry?

I stood up quietly and began to walk away as the other guys came back. "B-Boss," Alex said, "where are ya going?"

"To apologize," I said calmly.

"W-what?" Jasper asked with surprise, "who--why?"

As I continued walking Roger smacked Jasper at the back of his head and still heard them arguing when I got away from our park and I was looking around for Levia, maybe Lila if I'm really pushing it.

I decided to ask the she-wolf, Vulpa, where I should go in order to look for Levia. "She-wolf," I found her in the plaza eating some beef jerky. She glared at me for not saying her name, then tried to ignore me, "Vulpa," I said in defeat.

"Good enough," Vulpa tore into the piece of jerky and put it down, "are ya looking for the chick you scared off from your camp?"

I looked around uncomfortably, anxious if anyone was staring at us. "Yep…" I muttered.

"What for, bud?" she looked at me with concern, and asked quietly back.

"To apologize," I answered quietly, "I feel like an ass, making her cry an' all…"

Vulpa smiled and put change on her table as she stood up, not finishing her food. "They're prolly in the library," she told me, "but getting there is tricky," she wiped her hand in a paper towel while walking towards me, "I'll take ya there an' let ya in, bud." She threw the towel away and began to drag me by the arm.

"Oh, darn…" Vulpa broke the ice we went through after we left the plaza, "never learned your name… Fishsticks was it?"

"Did Birdbrain put ya up to that?" I asked, annoyed.

"Then how do you want me to call ya?" We took a turn and headed through a mossy area.

"My usual name is Gills," I answered cautiously, "but my actual name is Dylan Vann."

"Then I'll call ya…" we took another alley turn that was built with seemingly new bricks, "D.V."

"How did you come up with that?" I stared at her, baffled.

Vulpa snickered cockily. "You're a FH correct?" she walked me through her path of thought, "so that means you Dive a lot, right?"

"I don't know if I follow this…" I tried to lump the pieces of her explanation together.

"So D.V., like a DiVer, naa-ahh?" Vulpa was smirking at her genius.

I deadpan stared at her and mockingly laughed. "Incredible logic, Oh great Lady of Comedy."

"Oh, come on, D.V.," she poked me mockingly, "you know I'm a genius."

I smirked when we reached an ancient clockwork door. "Yeah-yeah, Lupa," I answered her with a smile, "you're the light of the future."

She touched the door while glaring at me. "My name is Vulpa, Fishsticks."

"Fair-fair," I conceded while the door steamed and clocking open.

Vulpa then led me through a few corridors, sniffing around thoroughly. After a few turns she stopped me and poked her head out of a corner. "Guess who came to say hello," Vulpa then shoved me to an enclosed and quiet area filled with tablets and scrolls.

Levia sat up when she saw me. I limply raised my hand and waved it stiffly. "I…" I started to admit my guilt, "came to apologize for making you cry…"

Levia smiled cheerfully. "You did that before too," she stood up and looked behind the wall of books, "it seems that the wolf has left…" She snickered, "she's pretty strange."

"Ya can say that again," I laughed with liberty, "but I wanted to apologize for my memory loss as well…"

Her smile became dry. "Yeah…" Levia put her cold and dry hand on my cheek, "something similar happened to Emile's partner as well…"

Lila pulled one of the scrolls and opened it. A flash of light sparked from it and an Image of a Bird Hybrid with strange and fancy clothes sparked to life. "Oh, hi Lila…" The lady looked distressed, "I see Levia's here too," she seemed to be looking through tons of paperworks, "and the Creator of Land as well…?" she looked directly at me, "don't tell me you don't remember sweet Levia, hmm?" The lady returned to look at her paperwork.

When she did, I admitted that… "it's true."

The woman was startled when she heard my answer. "Just like Ollie…"

"I guess…" then a realization came washing over me, "wait… did you just say- Ollie?" she nodded, I looked at Lila in puzzlement, "where's Ollie though?"

The lady, Emile, sighed in sorrow. "He's away for now," she explained, "but my friends don't want to tell me anything concerning him," she gestured to the piles of papers, "and being a God ain't easy I'll tell ya that."

I was flooded due to the info dump on my head and stared at Levia. "Are--" Levia silenced me with her pointer finger and nodded grimmly, "then what does that make me…?"

"My partner."

Levia smiled confidently, "and we're gonna locate where your memories are buried, hmm?"

Lila called for me and Levia to her office with a small piece of paper that was placed next to my sleeping bag. Levia was the one who found it next to it and she jumped up and down waking everyone up. We headed to Lila's office with my guys as they groggily conversed.

"Why are ya so excited to meet Miss Smith like that?" Roger asked, rubbing the rust out of his eyes, "she's not that different from the army cyborgs, no?"

Levia glared at him. "She IS different from them," she slapped the back of his head, "she has her own will to ignore mortal orders!"

"Meaning?" Roger held her hand.

She sighed in annoyance. "She's the older 'twin' of the Golden Creator," Levia explained, "and that Creator has been punished by the ancients that, in any world the the Six of the Natural Lords inhabit her birth will be split into 'twins', one older and the other, the younger will be born out of the misery of the eldest," she stopped for a moment as we reached Lila's office, and looked up desperately, "and once in that world cycle the eldest and youngest coexist, the loop repeats once more."

I stared at her. "How do you know all of that…?" I asked, puzzled.

Lila opened her office's door. Her robotic tail and wings were hung on the wall and she looked terribly ill. Levia ran in to support her. "Something's wrong," Levia said with alarm, "where's the head nurse?"

"He's… out for the moment…" Lila said through scrambling her speech, "however… Elijah can't locate him at all."

Roger's eyebrows raised in confusion but alarmed all the same. "Shouldn't you send folks to look for him…?" He wondered, heavily concerned while scratching his days-old stubble.

"Most of the kids here have no desire of looking for the guy," Elijah sparked up when Levia laid Lila to her bed, "and the nurses are not fully able to treat my Lady's condition, so the only person that can help isn't here as much as he's not wanted."

"What was his latest location?" I asked, "and as much as I can't trust the guy or the cyborg," I looked at the heavily breathing Raptor, "I want to help with whatever I can… since she does the same for the guy."

"Understood," Elijah opened a map of Russell's last location, it was in the middle of the no-man's-land seaside in the direction of the Western Unity sea, "I am unable to detect any further, apologies…"

"Thank you," I said and grabbed a portal orb that was next, "I hate to say this," I looked at my guys, "but that nurse is currently important to Lila's health, so we either take him back here or get his data in order to teach others," I turned to Levia, "I know you've just recovered from your waking, but---"

"Of course I'll help!" She cheerfully exclaimed, "since I know the ocean like the back of my hand, I'll be able to locate that wet ass weasel better."

Levia grabbed the orb out of my hand, brimming with confidence and activated it. The gang went in that portal before us and I stopped before going in. "Who are you, really?" I asked sternly, "how would you know the ocean like that…?"

She smiled reminiscently. "I can't explain that in a few words," Levia pushed me into the portal, then came in after me, "this'll be an *awfully* long story… it'll be easier if I show you a fraction of it…"

We were dumped around the middle of both no-man's-land territory and of the Western Unity. Levia headed to the nearest sedimentary rock and began meditating. "Umm--" Roger, puzzled, began to ask but I hushed him, "what is she doing?" he whispered instead. After five minutes Levia opened her eyes and looked at us and nodded grimly. We swam next to her as we went deeper into enemy territory. "The weasel abandoned the ship at his appointed time…" Levia sighed, "how disappointing…"

"What do ya mean by 'appointed time'…?" I asked her into her ear, no one else seemed to hear what she said.

She smiled a sad smile, as if she expected this question from me. "I told you a bit about the Loop of Creation, right?" Levia explained, I nodded, "so the way the world worked until now is that once the Golden Elder Soul Sister- Lila- lives alongside the Younger Soul Sister- Ms. Kaida- means that life will reset all over," she stopped us behind a rock and gestured for us to observe.

It was a small town of fish folks that was heavily monitored by soldiers and our weasel nurse was there, doing some testing and dismembering them and checking their healing factors as if they're normal sea animals. "Our people are in trouble," Levia spoke with a whisper, we stared at her, "and that weasel is clearly helping 'em."

"So our plans are to capture the guy and save the folks here, right?" Roger whispered excitedly.

Levia shook her head. "They're under the Unity's authority," she explained, "so we need to be more cautious and subtle with our approach."

We swam around to survey the outskirts of the shambled ruins of this town and saw a place to kidnap the weasel, it was a trash dump that was filled to the brim with broken limbs and tools which all but had lost their purpose. We hid and waited with bated breath and an opportunity rose. I grabbed the weasel, and he quickly began to struggle. Levia shushed him as we torpedoed back to the rock we started to survey the area then Levia created ice chains around the nurse.

"W-w-what?!" he grumbled, "H-h-how did you find me?!"

Levia held a tuft of fur triumphantly. "With this," she waved it with pride.

"W-when did you get that?" Russel asked with fear.

"Oh, I got that when you tried to intersect Lila, Dylan and I," Levia explained with confidence.

The weasel's eyes widened like saucers with surprise. "Y-you knew?" He asked in bewilderment, "you… who are you, Missy?"

Levia smiled serenely. "Someone that you should be worried about," she told him, then turned to me, "I believe we need some leverage over the nurse…"

I smirked and turned to the Ass. "I can suffocate all of your allies with a flick of my finger," I told him, concentrating on his oxy-tank as he began to huff and puff, trying to breath.

"O-okay, okay!" He struggled to speak and I stopped the atmospheric pressure, he sighed in relief, "fine," the weasel crudely answered, "I'll safely assume you came all the way here for a different reason than sabotage, aren't ya?"

"You are right," Levia continued, "Lila's in a bad shape, and you're out here, doing research on *my* people?"

"What's your line code?" Russel asked her.

"Why should I?" she answered with a curt tone.

"Because-" The weasel explained, "I would be able to delete your existence from the filing here."

"Are we supposed to believe the vagabond head nurse?" I told him.

He sighed a defeated exhale, then looked up at us. "Lila was the one to send me here," the nurse told us, "no one's supposed to know that the research to help everyone is this… appalling."

"Then…" Roger spoke up, "those guys here…?"

"They're with Lila's Covert Unity," he explained, "which means they report to Miss Smith first and the Western Unity second," he explained as Levia released the icy chains he checked his arms for frostbites, none could be found so he calmed down, "there are others that Miss Smith hires from inside the army, to keep tabs on the chaos if you will," he guided us into a hidden pathway that the test subjects don't go through often. But unfortunately one of the subjects found us.

"L-Lady Levia?" a young jellyfish man floated by due to a current, "are you going to be okay with this sick nurse?"

Levia smiled reassuringly. "I'm sorry I can get ya all out of this situation---"

"We agreed to stay here from birth to death," the jellyfish said, "that's just how we are…"

Levia grievely smiled. "I'm sorry--"

"Your highness," the man bowed, "we don't regret being here," he explained, "and, nurse…" he looked at Russell, "I overheard what you told Her Majesty…" he stuttered, "so… our suffering helps others… right?"

"Indeed it is," the nurse finally spoke, "but make sure the soldiers don't know that you know… you might be sent elsewhere--"

"I cannot leave this place," the jellyfish explained, "the reason we fought you, is that fact that this land is sacred to us, the folk that live here…"

"This land is connected to each life that's born here," Levia calmly clarified to Russell, "if they leave this place they'll die, with their souls becoming destructive, to a stage of Malice that can't be solved unless the body is returned to this place," she glared at the nurse, "if the soul isn't appeased at a week after death, it becomes a Nightmare and absorb every life force in the vicinity." Russell hurriedly told us not to leave with the data and gave us the crummy paper data, then left us in the cabin-like underwater facility and we read through it. It also had Lila's private diary deep amongst the pounds of paper.

Lila's condition was horribly grim, as her very being is diminishing for the last five years and only gotten worse in the last five months due to a death of someone important.

That someone was her old childhood friend and partner at her organization to rehabilitate refugees of the wars between the big three opposing forces and the place she rents for that was thanks to him reaching out to some higher ups in many places, not just the warring nations, and managed, together with Lila, to create a dimensional rift in order to protect the residents and patients.

His name was Eric Arbeider.

Due to a botched sabotage mission he was captured and in one way or another pronounced dead. His body lived through the same process used to create Lila, however since they improved the drugs and the mind control type Nightmares that completely erased who he used to be, due to his connection with Lila the Eastern Republic sent her a summons to have a chance to see him again, and to offer herself in order to send him to the organization's dimension.

Lila was aware of the fact it's a trap and planned together with Russell on a way to get him out safely -and- not get captured by the Republic's army. They planned to use the same rogue wire gun that Eric used on her and kept tweaking it to make sure it'll work on others like Lila.

But it failed.

When they met there was no one in his body, no memory of their friendship, a clean slate. Lila tried the gun anyways and when the army came to capture her she shot herself with the gun and amplifying her magnetic powers and fended them off and Russell secretly picked her mangled body and Eric's corpse and took them back to their organization but his mind was already gone to who knows where.

That's when her condition worsened.

Roger read the whole thing multiple times over. "This is bad…" he affirmed, "what-- what can we do…?" he looked at us, frantic, "h-how can we even help?!"

Levia took the data and read it over, brows furrowed deeper and deeper. "There's not much we can do…" she said, faltering and mumbling to herself, "we need to go to Ocean Fell city to make contact with the other Gods, hopefully we'll find a solution together…"

The four of us stared at her, wondering how to get there to begin with, since the God of that town is dead and all, as far as anyone's aware.

"I did die twenty five years ago," Levia explained, "but I now live as you lot know me now."

"Okay, okay, this is confusing as hell," Roger tried to piece that information but I just placed my hand on his shoulder and shook my head.

"I don't get it myself," I told them, "but we'll have to just skid over this confusing information and head where she tells us, aight?"

They all agreed with me and scanned what was necessary for a prevention of her condition getting worse and sent it to the temp head nurse to take care of and headed out to the city Levia mentioned- Ocean Fall.

SHAUNA LEE; GUARDIAN OF DISEASE-

A servant girl knocked on my door and I answered it with a smile. "M-- my lady," she curtsied, "would you like some breakfast with Lord Behemoth…?"

I sighed and looked at the wardrobe in the room, filled with dresses. I was still wearing the disgusting clothes that still had my blood on them. "Can I clean up first?" she nodded profusely and when she headed inside to grab a dress before I shook my head, "I don't feel safe in a dress."

She looked awfully puzzled and dug through the wardrobe and pulled a pair of long and navy blue dress pants and a nice white frilly buttoned up shirt. She then went to the bathroom and started preparing a bath for me with intoxicating scents of bathing products. After she went out of the bathroom I soaked in the warm soapy water, washing away the grime and blood I've been walking in for three days now. I dressed up and the servant helped me with my shoe.

She then stood up and guided me to a small dining hall that was different from the dinner hall that was large and opulent. It was cozy and humble, with carpets on the floor and walls. The lighting was warm with incandescent light bulbs that glowed like small fiery stars. The table which Terry sat besides was a medium sized black oak wood dining table with a quaint quilted map with forest embroidery with bushes and grassland, animals and birds were sewn like spots of color, it had moon and stars with true love to the person who gave this quilt to the manor's Lord.

"I see you appreciate this old thing," Terry gestured for me to sit next to him and quietly filled my plate with food, "an acquaintance of mine made it very, very long ago."

"It is very well made…" I sat next to him and began shoving scrambled eggs and bacon into my mouth, "it was made with honest love towards ya."

He chuckled. "The guy was about a hundo years old when he made this," Terry explained, "he is one of me boys ya know."

I was baffled. "Who---"

"We'll meet the guy today," he informed me, "what's wrong?"

I seemed to obviously stop eating and began to fidget the drawing in my pocket. "There's another person I wanna meet today…" I pulled the note out of my pants and showed it to him, he took it and looked at the crud writing, "can I meet her?" I asked cautiously.

Terry smiled reassuringly and cheerfully chuckled. "I don't see why not."

We finished breakfast and went to an open air auditorium and sat on the third line of seats as a rehearsal was operating. It was the birth of the God of Storytelling, the spider trickster Anansi.

Once there were no stories in the world. Kwanku Anansi the spider once went to Nyan-Kopon the sky god in order to buy the sky god's stories. A masked eight-limbed man began to narrate and approached a minimally dressed masked winged dragon man sitting on a throne.

"What makes you think you can buy them?" The dragon man inquired about the masked spider.

"I know I shall be able," Anansi answered.

The sky God chuckled dismissively. "Great and powerful towns like Kokofu, Bekwai, Asumengya have come and they were unable to purchase them, and yet you who are but a masterless man, you say you will be able?"

The spider began to ponder. "What is the price of the stories?" He challenged proudly.

"They cannot be bought for anything except Onini the python, Osebo the leopard, Mmoatia the fairy, and Mmoboro the hornet," the sky god admitted.

The spider stood brightly and proudly. "I will bring some of all of these," he began to walk away as the sky god challenged from behind him

"Go and bring them then!"

When they began the most interesting part the eight-limbed man pulled off his mask and waved two of his top arms at us. The dragon man noticed us as well, took off his mask and glided off his throne.

"Do ya already need a break, Anansi?" The dragon man asked.

Anansi took off towards us, ignoring the man as he made a beeline for the third row. "Popps!" He jumped over to Terry's lap, like a kid. He *was* the size of one though, but still. "You brought your ol' new Miss I see!"

"We take things slower than what Miss Milla planned to do," Terry told him, "we're not official y---"

"Oh gimme a break pops," Anansi cut him off, "what good did it give you during last Cycle, hmm?"

Cycle? What cycle?

"I don't want to force her ya know…" Terry tried to justify but the dragon guy added his opinion to the fray.

"You know what we mean, father," the man explained, "in the last seven Cycles you tried to take things slow," he looked at me with earnect sympathy and sighed, "she died before those Cycles, what would change this time, old man?"

Father…? Old man!? I know Terry's a God now, but I understand nothing in this entire conversation at all!

The dragon man noticed my puzzlement and hushed their arguments. "Aren't the two of us strangers to our dear Miss, Anansi?" The man bowed reservely and kissed the back of my scaly hand, "I'm Jabberwocky, or Jay for short--"

"Or JJ," Anansi cut him off, he scooted over next to my seat and whispered excitedly, "but he doesn't like it when people call him that," he hissed as he chuckled, very amused at himself.

"What's your name, Miss?" Jay asked me and sat in the second row in front, waiting curiously and patiently for my answer.

I kind of lost my voice for a moment and saw Terry nodding and reassuring me to speak. "M-my name i-is Shauna Lee," I told them, "b-but you can call me Tails because my human name's too weird…"

Jay and Anansi shared a look and glared at Terry. "You are aware that she might not have a tail once she passes the ceremony, right, old man?" Jay whispered to him, "if she'll last that long that is…"

OLIVER HARPER; CREATOR OF MATTER-

When we returned to the temple everyone was frazzled and terrified out of their mind and Tenku was barking orders at everyone. Emile pulled out a harp and strummed the strings with a loud and calming tune. Everyone calmed down in an instant. Everyone but Tenkubashi.

"Why did you bring the faker here, my Lady?" he glared at me, completely pissed off.

I thought of my instrument and summoned it forth, my trusty crwth and struck the strings and nodded to Emile as she played her harp in the tune of the Lullaby of the Nightmare Bane, the first song we ever wrote together. I don't remember when exactly or why, but it's a lullaby I know by heart. It was a tune and a story of the creation of earth with the other gods- the Mesopotemian, Meso-Americans, all the Afrikaans, Greek, Celtics, Nordic, Shinto, the Tao, the Hindu and last and incredibly unneeded 'singularity' of Yhwh.

When we finished Tenku angrily and gave me a feather-like emblem and left grumbling. Emile pulled a few strings and everyone at the temple calmed down and went to do their usual chores as the attendant that helped me bath three days ago and sheepishly gestured me to follow him to the dust baths and began to clean myself up.

The attendant clearly had some questions for me. I smiled and told him to ask away. "Wouldn't it be presumptuous of me to ask such questions," he timidly brushed my hair, "b-but--" he cut himself off and I kept quiet, but he took a deep breath and continued, "are you really the Creator of Matter?"

I snickered with amusement. "It has been surprising for the both of us, huh?" I answered him with a smirk, "don't be a stranger, aight?"

He nodded profusely.

Once we finished cleaning and I dressed with way more comfortable clothes, I heard a knock on the door and the attendant answered. "Lord Tenkubashi!" The attendant exclaimed.

I waddled to the door, pants still halfway up. "To what do we owe the pleasure," I asked calmly, pulling my pants up and letting the attendant leave my room, "O' Lord Tenkubashi?"

Tenku laughed. "I started on the wrong foot with ya," he explained, scratching the back of his head stiffly, "I just want to hang out, to get to understand ya better, alright?"

I smirked mischievously. "It's a date then?" came out of my mouth as I snickered, "I'll keep that between us."

Tenku glared at me with disgust. "Dude!" He began to laugh, "you're a strange one, aren't ya?"

"I think I'm still a bit drunk, bud," I told him, "maybe I need more to drink."

He chuckled. "I will try to sober you up, mister," Tenku put my arm on his shoulder and dragged me out of the room, "no more drinks for you, bud."

He took off with four wings as usual, out of the temple and he slowly let me glide below him, I then caught the wind and flew behind him, spreading two wings. I followed Tenku to a small but high class coffee shop. The hostess introduced herself to us and guided us inside a mostly full restaurant, patrons staring at us, then got seated in a quiet area with less people walking and talking.

The menu a waitress gave us was in Bird tongue and I did understand bits and pieces but not enough to understand what I wanted. Then Tenku just ordered for the both of us in Bird Tongue a fruit smoothie sweetened with honey and a breakfast sandwich for me and a complicated order of certain tea and cake that I didn't follow.

"I'm not your girl, ya know?" I said with a dreamy smile, "only if you want me to be," I snickered.

Tenku sighed uncomfortably. "Look at it as you want," he told me with an awkward stare, "but I invited you here to get to know ya, since you clearly have a bit of your memories back."

I sighed in acceptance that he wouldn't lean on my half drunk jokes. "Understood," I straightened up and got serious, "what would you like me to reminisce about?"

"Your life before you met Emile," he leaned closer, "I am curious what life you've led before."

I sighed bitterly. "I don't like talking about myself much…" I explained, "but, if you laugh at my story or judge my past I'll stop talking, understand?"

Tenku nodded affirmatively.

I told him about my history. I was conceived as a way for my mother to get a raise in order to take care of my older siblings. My mother became enamored with the idea of raising me herself, as a normal human child. Nothing would've stopped her when she ran out of the facility where I was born and raised me like a normal boy, hybrid or no, with my older human siblings. My siblings were marked as deceased when we escaped in order to protect them from retribution. I was treated fairly and justly by my mother and siblings and we all love each other even today.

But all happy things come to an end, and the army found us and captured my mother and I when we were buying groceries, so they never knew my siblings were still alive so the two of us were captured, while they were safe and working as nameless retail workers. When we were captured I started making the protective Image subconsciously and kept it pretty close while I was moved away from everything I've ever known and the moment of my first war I cut the Image completely off and locked every new positive memory away from me, sending the Image here.

When I was a teen I met Emile and we immediately hit it off, similar to Shauna and Terry, or Dylan and Levia. We've hung out together and partnered up for many missions for ten years. By the time the bigwigs realized that when we are together we're harder to control, they decided to split the six of us up to separate locations in the Unity's army facilities. But before they did the six of us designed a coup, uniting many under us including nurses and doctors.

We failed. The army used extra force to bind us and that's when I awakened, locking my memories with Emile away and going insane, consuming everything and everyone in my path. When I woke up I was in unimaginable pain and most memories wiped out but the pain I've caused to many, many people that were supposed to be my allies, and feared I consumed my friends. I was in a cavity of my own design and I decided to remain there and die of starvation.

That was when Lila and Eric, her partner, picked me up, unconscious and hungry. They nursed me back to health with the help of Russell, Lila's old nurse and now ally in more ways than one. That was when I realized I have a family that was worried about me and they were helping her to locate me and asked me to save our mother that raised me as her own human boy. I didn't have any memory of her, nor my siblings' faces and voices. I still saved them, not knowing why.

"And that's the end of the story so far," I took a bite out of the breakfast sandwich and a sip of my fruit smoothie, "I remembered more than before starting telling this story, so thanks."

Tenku was absolutely flabbergasted. "So that's why you were confused by her over-familiarity," he finally spoke up, "your partnership goes w-a-a-a-y back, huh?"

I finished chewing my sandwich bite and swallowed. "Apparently," I indifferently answered, "but it's probably longer than that."

"Meaning?" Tenku bobbed his head with curiosity.

I finished my sandwich and sighed. "My connection with her is longer than I can remember," I smirked as I sipped my drink with a cocky wink, "and so are you."

He was taken aback. "What?" was his only answer.

"You are the only one that can calm down both Emile and I," I explained, "when we get *really* mad…" I played with the straw, "like to a stage of 'destroying-everything-in-the-world' type of mad, ye see?"

"I didn't think I'm the type of person to be able to do that…" Tenku rubbed the back of his head awkwardly, "how would you know that?"

"Gut feeling," I told him with complete honesty.

Tenku looked doubtful at me. "How can you trust that?"

I chuckled. "I just do."

After we finished our meal and headed back to the temple awkwardly fluttering most of the way as Tenku glided to the empty park I stayed at not that long ago. The statue at the center was defaced and smashed to pieces. Tenku was more distraught than me when seeing this.

"Who…?" He kneeled down and was trying to piece the rubble back to a shape, "why…?"

"I guess someone *really* hates me right now…" I said with a matter of fact tone, "I will assume it's either the current dethroned mayor's family," I kneeled down myself and rested my hand on his shaking hands, "or yours."

Dylan Vann; Divider of Lands-

Three of my guys headed back to the organization while Roger and I stayed behind and planned our path to Ocean Fall and how to even locate the place, since the god has been gone for twenty five years. We planned our food and sneaked a few rations from the settled soldiers and hunted a few fish and shellfish for fresh food. Levia sat on the seafloor and started to prepare the fish with crystallized salts from the sea around us and gave pieces for us to carry and munch on while we swam around looking for the Husk that the city is placed on.

The Husk always moves around so locating the thing will take a while, so the three of us swam close to the floor looking for whatever would help us track it.

"So…" Roger swam slightly above us, "what are we looking for, Livi?"

She dug through the sand, sifting thoroughly through the sand. "A large and icy scale," Levia finally told us.

"Define 'large'?" Roger barked back swimming closer to the seafloor digging through the sand, "like as large as a bottle cap or the size of an arm?"

Levia chuckled. "The latter," she curtly answered as she kept digging.

He grumbled with annoyance at the fact that something that big wouldn't be *that* hard to find as we swam, looking for the thing.

"Why are we looking for the scale in the first place?" Roger wondered, puzzled.

She turned, glaring at his question. "The same way we located the nurse, ya know?" Levia curtly answered.

Roger quieted down and continued his search.

After swimming around I saw a glowing fish, very similar to the one that guided me to Levia's pod, and knowing that glowing fish have the habit of helping me I followed the fish and after a while of following it the fish stopped above a normal looking spot, so I dug there and found the scale Levia mentioned. The scale was as large as Levia's arm, clear like ice but strong as a diamond.

I looked around and realized I swam so far from Levia and Roger, further enough that I apparently had gotten lost. Well, drat…

I looked about for the portal orb I had but then recognized that Levia had it last time so I don't have a way to go back to the organization as well.

Then the ground shook and a giant and beautiful fish dug out of the sand and opened its enormous maw. That was when Levia and Roger caught up to me, their mouths agape.

"What is that?!" Roger exclaimed, "is it going to eat us?!"

Levia's lips were agape for a few moments longer. I could tell something was wrong. "This is the Husk!" she finally said, "what is it doing here?!"

Sea-folk soldiers swam out of the maw and from behind them I saw their leader, dressed like a high priest with all white with purple and adorned with gold and jewels. "I see the Creator came with the Faker and a stranger to these lands," he finally spoke while swimming towards us and taking the scale from my hands, "you're very welcomed here, Creator," soldiers cornered Levia and Roger, "but those two are to be questioned."

I got separated from Levia and Roger and was led in a different direction then them, and was led unshackled while they were both chained and forcefully led by the soldiers that met us.

"My dear Creator," the priest told me, "you're finally home with your true partner, with I--"

I scowled, but continued to listen.

"As the direct descendant of Master Leviathan themselves," he continued, "I was chosen to lead the Sea-folks to a better, brighter future by destroying humanity and returning the world into the primordial origins---"

I cut him off. "Isn't that extreme?" I confronted him, "I am aware humanity is filled with bastards, but there are a few good eggs there--"

He silenced me with a finger on my lips. "A few good eggs are late to rot," he shoved an orb in my mouth and I began losing consciousness, "you are meant to be my partner, not hers, understand?---"

Light enveloped me.

I woke up in a soft bed in an opulent room, decorated with glowing algae and corals, gold silver and white light bubble bulbs floated around the room. I glanced to the side of my bed, on the bedside dresser there was covered up and steamed dish. I sat up and picked up the dish. Under the cover was steamed fish dumpling with seaweed and nuts salad.

I closed the cover and got off the bed, studying this room I ended up in. Swam in front of the mirror and saw that I was stripped down to my birthday suit. I bolted and looked through the closet behind the mirror and saw there wasn't much 'clothes' in there if those could be called that.

I took the longest waistcloth I could find and paired it with the most covering scale harness, then covered it up with the most opaque silk robe I could manage.

A knock on the door, then burst open with the priest bolting in and looking at me, surprised that I've covered myself up like a sea-bug cocoon and approached me with a playful smirk. "Why are you covering up, my dear partner?" he asked me with a sleazy grin and shoved me to the bed and pushed me down to the covers, he began taking the very skimpy clothes off me with a flirty gaze. I couldn't take it and kicked him in the chest.

"Wh--what in hell do you want from me?!" I shouted, grabbing my clothes and putting them back on.

"You are to be my partner, dear," he grabbed my hand and forced a kiss on my clavicle, which made my body weak, "so we need to consummate this partnership, in the physical matter," he traced his long finger on my chest, giving me bursts of... vile pleasure, "and it must be done as quickly as possible--"

I pulled what little strength I had left and kicked him off again. "I-I don't want this," I uncharacteristically whimpered, "can we take some time… before all this?"

He looked at the dresser and scowled. "You haven't eaten, have you?"

"Why would I?" I told him in my personal cold demeanor, "I can't trust it for it to not be drugged."

He turned back to me with an annoyed gaze. "Why would I do that, darling?"

I put some clothes back on. "Point proven," I absentmindedly took the dish and threw it in the trash, "I can't trust ya, 'darling'."

I dashed out of the room I was assaulted in, and began looking for Levia and Roger's whereabouts. I swam around the giant temple area as far away from that thirsty priest as I could. A glowing fish caught my eye, and from my experience of those fish and guiding me towards positive things, I decided to follow it around with the Hope of being guided to my old friend.

Levia… Just be okay…

The fish took me through back rooms and hidden doors and pathways until I arrived at a very dimly lit cave corridor maze, continuing to chase that fish until I heard a voice singing an old nursery rhyme. I approached in the direction of the voice and reached a solitary door with a small window the size of a wall mirror. Levia was sitting on a rough coral bed, bruised and chuffed, singing a song I guess was long forgotten.

"L-Levia…?" I whispered to my dear friend, "what's going on?!"

Levia stopped singing with a startle. "Dylan…?" She came to the door in a gleeful but puzzled rush, "how did you find me?"

I cocked my head to the side, confuzed. "I thought you were guiding me all along," I explained, "the glowing minnows guided me to your location so far…"

She looked puzzled, calculating. "Your past self might've made them to guide you…" Levia mumbled her thoughts clearly, "but this Cycle is off this time…"

I peered into her face. "You mean this didn't happen before?"

Levia looked back at me with crystal-like tears and quietly nodded. "That priest was supposed to recognize the both of us and give up this chase for control…" she told me with a thoughtful stare, "but he became corrupted by the children of Lust and Greed…"

I stared at her, not knowing what that even meant.

"You need to help Roger build a purification device and play as a confuzed victim while you do," Levia told me, "don't eat the food he gives you to your room and only eat with the other servants, understood?"

"Are you okay with that?" I asked her.

"Open for a moment," she told the door as it clicked open and she cupped my cheek in her cold hand, "Dylan… may I kiss you…?"

I stared in surprise. "Why would you want that--"

Levia cast down her eyes. "It's to take the bond breaking orb out…" She excused it to me, looking back up, "so…"

"If it means that the bastard won't force me to fall for him," I smiled reassuringly, "I would want no one else's tongue in my throat."

Levia chuckled and kissed me, shoving her tongue heartily down my throat. I couldn't breath, but felt the pleasure of our bond. The moment she was trying to pull away I grabbed the small of her back and kissed her back. She was tensely surprised as she softened and gave herself to my… love…

Love, huh? Did I always love her…? Is it because we were destined to be partners, or is it my own will?

Once we reluctantly separated she let go of me and returned to her jail. She smiled behind the window and swam back to her rough bed and began to sing again.

I know what to do. I will succeed.

Shauna Lee; Guardian of Disease-

After they finished their rehearsal Jay and Anansi changed their stage outfits and came to meet with me and Terry to have a chat.

"So Shaun wants to meet with the head of the Itachi clan?" Anansi wondered, "it may sound like a piece of cake to meet her, but she doesn't like talking to strangers outside her clan."

I grabbed Katerina's drawing and pulled it out to show them. "If so," I smiled cheekily, "that might help."

Anansi stared at the drawing with an intense stare. "How your childhood dr--" then realization set in, "it actually might help ya, Shaun!"

Jay came and noticed the same thing as Anansi. "We should head over right now," he told the three of us, "if you don't mind, popps."

Terry nodded reassuringly. "The more the merrier," he smiled at me, "am I wrong, Shauna?"

I smiled and nodded in agreement. "I'll take any help I can get," I told them. We then headed through the heavily populated streets, getting stares and glares from everyone. I believe they mostly stared at the storytelling stars that were walking around with Terry and my misshapen ass. The people that glared were very human looking and those that stared at us were homeless people that had my condition.

Those that tried to glance away were awkward parents with children that move out of the way to make sure the kids don't stare.

A cat hybrid looking seventeen years old was discreetly shoved into an alleyway, one that the four of us were about to move past but I stopped in my track. I could tell the girl was distressed and I was about to follow the poor girl when Anansi put his hand on my shoulder.

He turned my body to face him, his eight beady eyes filled with worry and alarm. "You want to help that girl on your own, right?" Anansi stared intently, "you *really* shouldn't---"

Jay cut him off and disappointedly shook his head. "You know it ain't gonna stop her, right partner?" he told Anansi in defeat.

Terry looked at me, heavily concerned with furrowed brows and a stern lip. "Do you really want to help that girl?" he asked me to affirm my choice.

I nodded quietly. "She's in a similar situation to me," I told the three of them, "I would like to help her…"

Terry showed me a sad smile. "You know I'll have your back now, alright?" he asked me gently, "if you need our help, shout--"

Anansi cut him off when he spit a string of web, extending it, tying it to my waist and giving the other side to Terry. "You know why, Pops," he coldly told Terry.

I then headed into the alley taking deep breaths and looking ahead, determined. I heard the girl's soft heart cries as she laid there naked and the putrid alley water and the two men taking their own clothes off. When they were about to take their boxers I yelled for them to hold it.

At the moment they heard my voice they almost jumped out of their skins, but when they noticed that I was a hybrid like the girl they tried to screw, confident smirks appeared on their faces as the shadows of the backstreet made them as menacing as Cobra was back at the facility.

Hungry, like terrifying beasts in human skins.

"Why would someone disgusting like you care about another filth?" One of the beasts said, licking his lips.

Vile and disgusting, the rot of the alley fits those two.

The other bastard placed his hand on my deformed shoulder chuckling proudly all the while. "You're *clearly* jealous of that kitten," he began to cockily unbutton my shirt.

Memories flowed back, the helplessness, the guilt, the disgust. That was when my brain went- *OH--NO-NO-NO, OH HELL NAW--*!

Then I grabbed his arm, kicked him in his crotch and smacked my knee to his face breaking his nose with a deafening crunch, my pants were smeared with the vile man's nose. The man crumples to the ground in pain holding his face, crying in pain. "Bitch…" his friend said, "no one told us that you're such a bitch!"

"Told you?" I looked around, surveying the area for observers but saw none, "who told you about me?"

He cockily chuckled. "Why should I tell ya, vile reptile?" he cursed me under his breath, "I have no clue why you'd be interested in helping a prostitute that was just doing her job, but that's beyond me---"

The guy was cut off by a shot from a gun. I instantly coiled into a ball and began to shake violently. Terry, Anansi and Jay ran in with weapons ready, surrounding me. Terry sat next to me when Anansi checked the guy and noticed that the kitten I tried to save was holding that gun, standing up, holding the gun and putting on a familiar cloak of an Aslan assassin while holding the gun.

"Do ya think you want to threaten Lord Beast's direct partner while he's right here, Missy?" Anansi intimidated the kitten, pointing at Terry.

"I wasn't told that His Majesty would be here---" she glared at Anansi, "you're lying, aren't you, Bug?"

"I'm a spider you dounce!" Anansi exclaimed but was hushed by Terry.

Terry stood up, glared at her with intense flames in his eyes. "You'd want to run that by me again," he cautioned her quietly.

She stared at him, baffled. "And you are…?"

Terry boomed in ironic laughter. "Are you a new recruit, Miss?" he glared coldly at her, "have you been caged before getting to be sicked on my partner, not knowing what I even looked like?"

She stared at the three of them, piecing the situation up in her mind. Then when realization hit her, she hurriedly tried to run away to the rooftops but her legs were stuck in Anansi's web.

"We're going to ask a few questions of ya, Missy," Anansi told her, "even if you don't know more than our Shauney's status."

"We'll still see what the Clan is up to," Terry said as he put his hand on her forehead as a green glow came out of it.

Anansi and Jay ushered me out of the alley and gave me bottled water with a straw as I was shaking uncontrollably. During the whole interaction I was hyperventilating and shaking like crazy.

Anansi and Jay had a talk while I was getting calmer and calmer.

"We might've been lucky to be here with Shauney this time," the spider voiced with worry.

Jay was rubbing my back quietly to calm me down a bit more. "Don't talk about this when she's right here, partner," he glared at Anansi, "you know it wouldn't change them, right?"

Change what? This cycle thing?

Terry finally came back out of the alley as calm as can be and ushered us to head for the Underbloom University's lab where Katerina's sister conducts research for a cure for her sister.

We went through more populated areas, not minding the stares and glares, as we finally arrived at the entrance of the university and freely headed to the laboratories' section. We reached a common room-like area and I was dragged to the receptionist by Anansi, not being let to soak the whole place in.

Terry approached the receptionist and slammed his hand on the desk. "We need to have a meeting with Miss Sabrina Itachi," He practically demanded, not carefully either, "is she willing?" Terry sneered.

The clerk calmly took a look at us, Terry's companions, from Jay to Anansi then me. "You, Master Beast might not be wanted there," he told us calmly, "the girl might be a point of interest to Lady Sabrina," the clerk gestured for me to follow him as I looked at Terry who sighed in defeat and became calmer the instant the clerk told me that I get in, Anansi was flailing four of his arms and gesturing thumb ups with the other two with an approvingly grin.

After a long while of walking through repeating walls and doors we finally reached Sabrina's lab door and was told to knock three times as loud as I could. I heard a saccharine sweet 'come in' that unsettled me badly but slowly opened the door anyways and got welcomed with a binder to my face. I picked it up, rubbing my hurting forehead and took a look at the cover.

The Strange Development of the Incomplete Folks / by R.C.

"Huh…" I absentmindedly mumbled, "why do those initials sound familiar…?" giving her the binder back with a puzzled look on my face.

"I'm so, so sorry for my welcoming binder to your face," the aggravated scientist apologized profusely, "I thought you were my mother…"

I chuckled quietly. "That's still a terrible welcome to anyone…" I whispered, "I wish my family came knocking sometime…"

She cynically laughed. "You wouldn't want a family like mine," Sabrina smiled with resentment, "after all, they kicked out the most powerful heir out of the family due an incredibly small failure."

I pulled the drawing Katerina gave me out of my pocket. Sabrina stared at the piece of paper I was straightening. "Is-- is this what I think it is?" she pleaded, "can I see a look at it with my two hands…?" I gave it to her and she carefully traced over the cheerful crayon lines and the character's gleeful smiles, "h-how do you have this?" Sabrina turned the paper over and quietly read the message in the back many times.

"She was sent to kill me," I told her, "your sister gave it to me before she left…"

Sabrina continued to hold the drawing with care for dear life. "M-may I keep it…?" She pleaded, "I want to give it back to Katt once I successfully find a solution for her, is that alright?"

I nodded reassuringly. "Sure thing," I affirmed her plea, then I sat down on a testing chair and crossed my legs, "the clerk probably took me here for a different reason I presume."

Sabrina gently folded the picture and put it in a desk drawer. She came to me, crouched down and cupped my hands with hers and cheerfully bounced, giggling. "You're a peach, you know that?" She stood up and brought equipment to take my blood for testing. She pricked my scaly arm with a wide needle and tried to start small talk with me.

"So… what's your family like, Miss?"

I wryly smiled. "The thing is… I don't know," I curtly answered.

Sabrina didn't get the hint. "Family issues then?" She pushed, "what about your mother, father, siblings…?"

I forced myself not to squirm in discomfort. "I don't know any of them," I told her as conceited as I could, "my mother died while carrying me, and I don't know my father if anything."

Her eyebrows rose in confusion. "What do you mean by that?" She wondered quietly, "Reptile mothers shouldn't die from carrying a child…"

"She wasn't a Reptile…" I blurted out, "she was a human that was sold to the army---"

"Our army doesn't--- oh…" realization hit her and she quietly finished taking my blood samples and got to the centrifuge and stared at it with uneasiness.

"Can I ask you a question?" I tried to break the ice and she turned to me and nodded cautiously, "I would like to know what my venom combination's like."

"Why would you want to know that…?" She asked, leaning on her desk, "buy I will be honest that now you mentioned it, nowI am curious as well."

Sabrina took a small venom extracting glass can, I took a tooth out, pressed it on the vinyl and filled it to the brim. I gave it back for her to test and she did give me another can and while I was filling it she tested the contents and told me her finding dumbed up for a non science person like me.

"There are hemotoxins which affect the blood cells causing their destruction and coagulation, dendrotoxins that usually paralyze any type of muscles, also myotoxins that cause horrible necrosis," she stopped to explain the toxins to me and glared at the screen then I came next to her and joined to the staring on the screen, I understood even less than her, "this… this is a hybrid type of genome modification drug and carcinogens…" she took a notepad and began to furiously scribble, while mumbling that more research is needed and I decided to quietly leave her to her devices.

The clerk that brought me here cheerfully grinned and took me back to the entrance babbling all the while about her genius and that he doesn't understand why she researches *my* type of people and further evolution and I lost him until we arrived at the entrance and met the guys. The clerk returned to his desk replacing his replacement and told me I'll get a call from the lab in the near future and bid me farewell, turning away an old woman that was claiming to be Sabrina's auntie but got denied, being told off and the lady turned and noticed us.

"Lord Behemoth!" she exclaimed, approaching us with aggravation that only an old lady can have, "can you believe that my own daughter turns me away like that?"

"As a matter of fact," Terry told her with shallow sass smirking all the while, "I do," he chuckled, "she hates ya with a passion."

I giggled quietly with agreement. "I can attest to that," I smiled cheerfully, "but you already know that, don't cha'?"

"You sure think highly of yourself, aren't you Miss?" The lady stared at me, puzzled, "why would you know of my daughter's thoughts of me?"

"Well," I averted my gaze awkwardly, "I just went to be tested by Sabrina, to help her on her research ya'know?"

She looked at me, dubvious. "How come you know what my daughter researches…?" She wondered and looked up to Terry and the others, "why are you here, your Highness…?"

"I brought my darling partner to help Sabrina's research," Terry hugged me from behind with a deadpan glare.

Her eyes went wide. "So it's true...?" She looked from me to him back and forth, "the Aslan family's fall from grace, huh?"

... Cycle... The Cycle... What is different this time, huh...?

"What did I say wrong, your Highnesses...?" The old lady snapped us out of our confusion, "I'm thoroughly apologizing if I brought any disrespect..."

"Don't think of it too much," Terry told her, his breath right next to my ear, as if he's talking to me more than to her, "You... what changed?"

The old gaff looked at his eyes with confidence. "I've had a visit from the Capricious Ancient," she told us with a cheerful smile, "She changed my mind about the Imperfect-folks and, at the time, tried to change my mind on my daughter's research--"

Whack!

A binder to the back of the lady's head. "Oh, hello there dear," the old woman calmly turned to pick up the binder, "is that a new research paper of Russell Catwalk?" She asked with a matter of fact tone.

"Nice of you to notice, Mother," Sabrina brusquely answered, "what are you still doing here?"

"Talking to your biggest supporter here," the matriarch answered with an offhand tone, "also," she gave Sabrina her binder back, "your fiance broke your engagement, in case you were worried."

Sabrina was taken aback by the news and took the binder from her, eyes and maw were agape, bewildered with eyes and maw open like the moon. "Why would an old weasel like you, would come all this way to inform me of this good news?" she bluntly asked her mother, "couldn't you have waited until I got back to the manse?"

An old weasel, huh...?

"Did you know that Russ is a weasel?" I absentmindedly interjected in their conversation, getting expectant stares from the two women.

"WHAT?!" The two asked with surprised grins.

I'm so sorry, Russ… What have I gotten you into… haha…

OLIVER HARPER; CREATOR OF MATTER-

"My family definitely would do something like that…" Tenku straightened up, eyes filled with burning rage, "after all, I'm but a pawn to them. Raised with the purpose to be a puppet ruler, an Eiji doll to them, planning my entire future since I was conceived," he looked at me, crying with pure broken rage, "while the Creator was glorified, I was told that I looked exactly like him, that I am probably his incarnation, putting me on a pedestal and showered with praise and admiration," he gently picked up the rubble and blew the crusty dust with tenderness,

"but when I found this park, I knew that I wasn't your incarnation, after all- you existed before me- I understood that my place was not to *be* you but *assist* you instead. I then was indoctrinated for years after that the statue I found was of my helper, that he was nothing compared to me and had no power over anything, that you were nothing but a slave- but the moment I heard you sing that dead song that only ancients are allowed to remember and sing- I knew *I* was nothing but a helper, that *I* had no power over anything---"

I hugged him and let Tenku cry with all his might. "Before Emile came here I was betrothed to the senator's vile daughter, had to always save face and rebelled by befriending the common folk in order to stay as far away from the entire family as I could," he continued blubbering,

"when Emile came, I wanted to help her- not because she was Ziz's incarnate, but because she was a lost soul like me being forced into a world we had no desire to live by its rules supporting each other as friends and not partners.

But when she turned to her true form I couldn't have been happier for her, but realizing what it would bode for the both of us- an arranged marriage will be forced down our throats- but I didn't want to force her, so I made a deal with her- I would be her consort on word to mouth but never married on paper."

"The family continued to pressure us but she told me to wait for you- the True Creator and not his descendant like me, that you would help us to be free of my family's rules and bonds," he looked up at me, "I trust you, buddy," Tenku sat up rubbing his puffy face, "don't tell anyone about this breakdown, aight?"

I gave him an acknowledging smile and helped him up. "You are aware Emile will know about this whether we like it or not?"

He sheepishly laughed. "I bet she would, after all- she's a God…"

We flew back to the temple when we saw a huge mob of raging nobles, from the senators to the Tenkubashi Clan slamming and shouting for Ziz to marry the *True* Creator, who is the heir to the Tenkubashi name, Eiji Tenkubashi and kick out the *Fake* Creator that just appeared and plans to dethrone high society pride to the gutters.

I looked at Tenku, eyebrows raised when he sheepishly told me that his birth name is Eiji, no less than an heir to his entire clan, though he felt more like a puppet than as someone that has a say for his own life.

I pulled my crwth with determination and told him to prepare his instrument for the Song of Destruction. He looked at me with worry. "You are sure about that, aren't you," he confirmed with me, "do you know what happens when it's played here, right?"

I nodded, affirming my desire.

The song was played, the Stone Guardians that were set all around the temple began to move, dust and moss fell off their limbs like rusty snow. From the first outside gardens to the front of the temple building itself, the statues were heading towards the 'noble' mob playing trumpets and beating drums.

While the smaller noble houses booked it at the moment we started to play the song the first senator house members and the Tenkubashi stood against the Guardians to fight, while the higher class members bolted to the temple doors when Eiji and I landed in front of them and strummed the wind at them.

When we stopped the song they were all captured, the Guardians locked the mob in their arms and claws struggling against their new stone chains.

"Eiji dear?!" a woman called for Tenku with an astonished cry, "what in the heavens are you doing with the faker?!"

Tenku sighed in defeat. "You are aware you made *me* the fake, right?"

The woman gasped in appahling surprise. "HOW DARE YOU?!" She glared at him, stretching her neck like an emu, "DO YOU KNOW WHAT WE'VE BEEN THROUGH TO GET *YOU* WHERE YOU ARE NOW?!"

Tenku went silent. I put a comforting hand on his shoulder but he went inside. "Trust me," I turned to head inside, Guardians slowly headed after me with the chained head of the mob screeching next to my ear, "he knows."

She huffed with indignation and pride. "Then you don't need me to tell you to go away from here, right?" the crow lady screeched.

"You really don't," I agreed, "but," I raised my hand to hush her, "everything you've done will be punished accordingly."

"WHAT?!" she screeched, "I'M EIJI'S MOTHER, I HAVE RIGHTS!"

I sideways glared at her. "Oh, you have rights," I chuckled, "but none will be given back until you leave your son to be his own man."

"HOW--"

AH~AH~AH!!

A curtl voice resaunded when we arrived at the doors of the main hall, Emile was sitting on her throne all dressed up with all the finery and gold of a high being, Tenku stood behind her when I glided and stood next to her throne. "You're all vile clan members," Ziz spoke up, "what do you have at your defense?"

"I'M EIJI'S MOTHER!" She screeched at us, "I DID EVERYTHING FOR *HIS* FUTURE AND SUCCESS! I sighed an exasperated sigh. "I believe that you don't lie in your belief, Ma'am," I said respectfully and calmly, "but Tenku has his own opinion on the matter," I nodded to him while he hid behind Emile's throne, and he squirmed to hide more efficiently.

Emile glared at the prideful mother and screeched back. "CAN'T YA TELL HE DOESN'T WANT ANY OF THE SUCCESS YOU WANTED FOR HIM," she cleared her throat and calmly continued, "you pushed him further and further for your desired success, you might as well not have him be his own being by now, hmm?"

The woman's eyes widened like an owl's glare but said nothing.

"Eiji," said a captured man, "won't you face your mother and I and say that to our faces, instead of this 'fake'?"

Tenku quietly whispered that he himself was the fake and not me.

"EIJI TENKUBASHI," his so called father called him as Tenku curled further, hiding his feelings from the overbearing parents, "COME OUT AND TELL US YOURSELF WHAT YOU WERE SAYING BACK THERE!"

I went behind Ziz's throne and extended my hand to him, encouraging him to finally stand up for himself. He looked up at me, his eyes puffy after crying and rubbing them off. "You can do it," I told him and getting to Tenku's eye level, "you are an adult now, aren't you?" I asked him softly, "Emile and I both have your back y'know," I helped him stand up and we both walked beside the throne holding hands.

"EIJI TENKUBACHI," the man sternly said with a scowl of disgust, "WHAT DID I TELL YOU ABOUT THOSE *FILTHY* DESIRE OF YOURS?!"

Tenku squeezed my hand due to the father's glower. I sighed, making the Guardian shut the man's trap hole. "You are aware he is his own being," I told the vile people calling themselves Tenku's parents, "not your doll to mold, understand?!"

"YOU 'FAKE' SHOULD LEAVE THE JUDGMENT TO *HER HIGHNESS*," the mother glowered at me, "your highness," she spoke in a saccharine sweet voice that made Tenku tremble, "you cannot allow your consort and the *fake* bastard be like this, now can you?"

Emile pierced her with a cold glare. "I approve of our courtmanship," Ziz finally spoke to the barn owl screecher, "you have no land or a piece of heaven that would bound you here," the egg donor opened her mouth to speak but was hushed, "they are my partners, through thick and thin they've been by my side never abandoning either of our bond," Ziz turned the Guardians into putty, and from it sealed them in them, "have I made myself clear?" she glowered at the other noblemen that stayed behind. They nodded profusely and were let go and they skedaddled away on fractured wings.

"Thank you," Tenku's knees buckled, "both of you," we both grabbed him from each side, "so much!"

DYLAN VANN; CREATOR OF STRATOSPHERE-

When I steeled my resolve for saving not just my dignity and self worth, Levia's reputation or Roger's freedom but the entire world as well. After all, he wants to drag life back into primal stagnation. I left the Labyrinth containing Levia's prison and looked around the courtyard and one of the soldiers near the entrance zipped over to me.

It was Roger, cheerfully skidding around. "What in the depths are you wearing?" He asked me while avoiding my eyes, staring at my clothes, "a-anyways--" Roger then took to grinning wildly, "even as an outsider, I was assigned to the head of the cybersleuth! I've been *blessed* by his Highness--"

I grabbed him by the arm and took him away from the earshot of his subordinates. "I need your help to purify the priest," I pleaded in a low voice, "you've learned the purifying process from Lila, right?"

Roger stared at me, confused. "Why would ya wanna do that?" he asked me with doubt, "isn't he your true partner or somethin'?"

"ABSOLUTELY NOT!" I hushed a grumble, "but he does want to force me into it, however--"

"Lord Creator?" A woman's voice came from behind me, desperate, "are you two able to purify my husband?"

Roger tried to deny it but the woman looked frantic.

"You want us to do it, right?" I bluntly asked her, she nodded, "you are aware he might die, you understand that?"

bewildered with eyes and maw open like the moon agitated. "I am aware of such a risk, Creator," the woman told us, skittish, "but let's talk about that somewhere private…"

The priest's wife took the both of us through quiet corridors and led us straight along coral walled garden walls and closed the door behind us and let off a relieved sigh.

She introduced herself as Tiamat Obscura, and her high priest husband as Gilgamesh Obscura, Gills for short. Same nickname as me… Even if I didn't have a reason to hate him before, I have one more.

"The moment Gills became the high-priest forty years ago he began to change. He was the kindest man I could ever know, warm and faithful, however he changed for the worst. He turned into an unfaithful, maliciously tenacious and cruel man, killing anyone who doesn't agree with his warped view," Tiamat explained the situation thoroughly, "he needs to be stopped, no matter how and for the greater good of the world," she told us with determination.

"The man tells everyone that he's the true Lord Fish, right?" Roger mentioned, mistified, "was that a lie…?"

"Obviously," I blurted out with venom seeped in this word, "I'm pretty sure of that, at least…"

"You are correct, Creator," Tiamat affirmed my suspicion, "this is a publicized lie he spread for the last twenty-five years - - -"

"That's how old Levia is!" Roger uttered, his eyes widened, "isn't that way later than the beginning of ol' Gills' corruption…?"

"That is correct," she saw the disgusted face I was wearing, "why would you make such a face?"

"Not only is he a corrupted bastard," I told them, bile rising in my throat, "he's also a vile sexual predator."

"WHAT?!" Roger's mind fog has begun to clear, "is that why you're 'dressed' this way to satisfy his sick perversion towards you…?"

"I, unfortunately, would assume so," Tiamat confirmed.

"I've heard that he's possessed by children of Greed and Lust, right?" I brought up, "how do we get them out of him, though?"

"The fact you are aware of that is impressive," Tiamat was taken aback, and excitedly continued, "I met the two when he became the high-priest, that was when he appointed them to be his personal bodyguards and punishers of all who opposed him."

"Now that's interesting," Roger remarked, "then we don't really gotta kill the guy, right?"

"Unfortunately, it's no longer a possibility," Tiamat disclosed to us, "the two Nightmares and my husband are inseparable now, so killing one will only make the others stronger and revive the perished…"

"It sounds like you've already tried that before, huh?" I got a glimpse of a glowing minnow, and started to follow it while we were still talking and they began to follow me.

"That minnow's glow…" Tiamat realized while we were chasing the little guide-fish," it's the same one that guided me to the two of you," she told us, "helping me escape the Low Tower cellar where I was sealed by my husband."

After many twists and turns further and further away from the public roads and streets, we reached the Rebellious Quarters. Rebels glared at us from every nook and cranny all around us. A dominant leader approached us with determination and pride.

"What brings the Traitor, a new leading outsider and our 'dear' Creator right to our clutches?" they demanded.

"To help y'all in your rebellion, of course," I confidently answered, unwavering, "are you disapproving of our assistance?"

"Why should I trust any o' ye?" The leader challenged us.

"Levia prevented me from being manipulated into submission to the bastard," I told them, "I've met her personally in her cell not that long ago."

"Do you have proof of that?" they questioned my legitimacy, "you're still wearing the submission dressing."

"Do you think I had the ability to buy my own clothes here?" I retorted, "I came from the human settlements with no dough to my name."

"You came from the human side?" a girl's voice pleaded from behind the leader, swimming into the spotlight, "do you know Mr. Roger from the Eastern Republic...?"

"That's me!" Roger raised his hand cheerfully, I stared at him in confusion, "B-Boss... you don't remember that you were the one that took me to the Western Unity's war prisoners camp?"

Strangely enough, I couldn't remember any of that.

"Mr. Roger calls Mr. Creator Boss?" The little girl looked up at me in admiration, "then I'll trust you, Mr. Creator!"

"Evie!" The leader bellowed at her, "do you want to hurt again?"

The girl, Evie, curled into a ball in fear. "N-no..."

"I don't know what'll change your mind," I pleaded, "but you can at least let me borrow clothes other than these slave auspices?"

"If we give you our robes," the leader explained, "you wouldn't be able to leave our sight in order to report to your lord---"

"O please do!" I wholeheartedly agreed, "I don't want to be anywhere near the bastard that tried to break my connection to Levia!"

The leader's eyes went wide. "You sure hate the man--"

"You have no idea how much I despise the guy," I hissed with venom seeping in me words, "if I get to be supervised by y'all instead of the thirsty jerk I'm all for it!"

After the looks of surprise from all of the rebels I was given a nice shirt, a leather jacket and pants to wear. When I was done Roger was gone and Tiamat had ropes with metal talismans on her neck and wrists.

"Oh, Creator!" she waved widely and loudly, noticing my puzzled look on my face, "oh, these?" Tiamat shook wrists, "don't worry, I got what I deserved, due to last time..."

"You look well, Creator," the leader approached me, cautiously still.

"Well, I have a name ya know," I finally got to properly introduce myself, "it's Dylan Vann or D.V for short, my pleasure."

The leader snickered and he began to relax around me. "Now that you're one o' us," she took my arm and dragged me around the block, "I usually call me-self as Ara, sometimes Kishin and less often than none as Sazan," Ara caught my stare, and giggled, "you can use those interchangeably, I don't care how you refer to me either way."

"I see…" I said, taken by surprise and confusion.

"Mr. Creator- Mr. Creator--" Evie zoomed right to me, "I want a piggyback- I want a piggyback!"

I took a cautious look at Sazan and got a confirming smirk. Evie glided to my back and held tight with both legs and arms around my chest and head. I tickled her a bit to let me both breath and see.

"Make sure you hide yourselves properly wherever ye go," Ara reminded Evie, "come back at the first sight of danger, understood?"

I saluted and headed towards being a taxi seahorse and she began to tell me directions and began small talk with me. "What do ye wanna be called as a code, since ye're a fugitive an' all?" she asked while we swam on the safer streets.

"Call me D.V., it's much shorter than my full name," I stopped and answered her, "how do we hide in the main market plaza…?"

Evie pulled on my shirt, apparently I had a hood shirt, and covered my head with it. She did the same with her shirt and gave me a thumbs up to continue.

"Is there some way I should act on the street?" I asked her before continuing, "because 'acting normal' is not in my vocab."

Evie pondered a bit. "Act like when you go on a sabotage mission?"

"Then alert stealth it is then," I took the first push into the streets.

She jumped excitedly on my shoulders. "Let's go to the Library," Evie told me with unashamed excitement at the prospect she brought up, "even though the one we have here is just a branch, there's limited access to every bit of Lady Knowledge's knowledge a bit every day."

While we continued our small talk, she guided me around people and food stands, shops and quite a few guards."What does it mean that the local library is just a branch?"

Evie's smile widened with glee. "It's no 'ordinary' library," she told me in a nerdy kind of joy, "it's a branch of THE Library of the ancient o' the concept of knowledge, she's usually referred to as Knowledge or Lady Knowledge."

I quieted down with a blank stare on the road. "You must realize the fact I have no idea what you're talking about, Evie," I told her when we reached the Library branch thing that we came in for, "I may be some kind of a 'Creator' or somethin', but that doesn't mean I'm omniscient and such."

We headed inside and got greeted by a skittish eldritch abomination, with tentacles swiping randomly and sharp gaping maws chiping in unison, that welcomed us in with an oddly normal voice. "If it isn't our little Evie and young D.V.!" It welcomed us cheerfully.

"How--" I was cut off by Evie as she asked what she came in for.

"Can we use the records room for the day?" She quietly asked the abomination.

"But of course dear Evie," the eldritch monster cheerfully told her as it pushed a few buttons and a lever, they became quiet," by the way, my brother, I'm Yog-Sothoth by the by."

Where have I heard this name…?

She just guided me away from my questions and led my oblivious ass to the records room. The room was filled to the top with stone tablets, metal scrolls, impregnated papyrus scrolls and digital-note-looking tablets.

Evie and I split and swam through the room, looking for interesting looking files. Evie and I exchanged files and sat down to skim through them. I picked up a digital-notebook and flipped through it. A question popped into my head while just skimming the thing-

Why am I understanding this language…?

The data recorded in there is the same way I write my journal, the name mentioned on top is Exo Daltone, or E.D. for initials that kept repeating in the journal.

A being called Mother seems to be the origin of the Tale of the Golden Twins' predecessor before the 'split', and she's the one who caused it. This world was given to us and so many other olde gods like Nunn, Gaia and Uranus, Izanami and Izanagi, so, so many others that got lost through the read.

The Creator of Matter comes first and creates a material base for most of the gods to start with their creation of the natural world, My predecessor, Exo, was tasked to create a habitable atmosphere that had to change multiple times due to gods' interference and squaballing over how many suns should be in the sky, or what materials humans should be created from, how should they worship etc… So humans had to happen with the help from the Creator of Life's predecessor because they had the main plan given to them by Mother and planned the human evolution thoroughly to make sure they have the correct consistency of being.

Unfortunately, humans eradicated other humans and began to follow the gods that took the credit of creating them through the ways that were told previously.

The Three Creators' partners, The Proud Fish, The Valiant Beast and The Benevolent Bird, created the folks that maintain their existence through the ignorance of Man.

Evie did notice I was reading the most ancient language file we could find and stared at me with awe.

However our peaceful reading had to come to a halt when I heard the bastard priest's voice booming through the entire Library like thunder at night.

"What do you mean that my beloved partner isn't here?!" He demanded, "I know he's here, I can feel it!"

"If you meant Lady Tiamat," Yog-Sothoth continued to ignore his tantrum, "she isn't here either--"

"I do not care for the sea witch of a traitor," the priest continued, "I have an informant who told me that my Creator is here!"

"And who might that be, Oh Great Priest?" Yog mocked him with a hearty laugh, "it's the Shaftri clan head, isn't he?"

"We are not obliged to answer this query," a different voice boomed through the walls, it was stricter and more pissed off, "now bring us to the Creator!"

"No," the capricious librarian, "he isn't here--"

I heard an agitated shuffle from behind the wall we stayed in and saw a snake slither around the corner of my eye and grabbed the stranger by the collar and shut his maw.

Evie stared at the guy in surprise and alarm, and quietly whispered. "We should leave, like, NOW!" She hopped back on my back and rushed me away from the entrance we came through and I noticed the muffled brilliance of a minnow and were guided through strange corridors that lit like turquoise veins like blood pulsing through them. Well... that's what Evie told me they looked like while I was chasing the minnow and reached the labyrinth Levia was held in.

I heard her singing and knocked on the door which opened to my touch.

I kicked the guy inside as she stopped singing and bound him up in icey threads, leaving his mouth free.

"What's that for, Faker?!" he glared at her, "how did we even make it here, Creator?!"

I shrugged and came inside, Evie was attached to my back like a sea pup.

"It seems that our biggest ally was turned..." Levia approached him, "into our enemy..."

"What are you talking about, you liar!" the man bellowed, he turned to me, "why would you trust a liar like her--"

I smacked the crown of his head and held his grimy hair. "Hard to believe that Levia called you an ally a minute ago," I glared into his eyes, I looked up at Levia, "it seems like he's in the same daze Roger was in when I met him and Tiamat when I ran from the priest…"

She hmmd and hawd and pulled some kind of serpent that latched to his soul and the man was knocked out. The serpent struggled and clawed at Levia when her eyes shone with icey light and froze the monstrosity into a beautiful slithery glacier statuette.

Levia then released the man from his glacier binds and crouched next to him, poking him repeatedly. Evie nervously jittered behind me squeezing my jacket till her knuckles turned white.

The man smacked her hand off his forehead and sat up yawning and stretching as if he slept for years. "Huh…?" he looked around the room, "what happened…?" the man stared at Levia, and held her hand that was still hanging in the water due to him hitting her, "I'm so-so-soooo sorry for disrespecting you by hitting you when you were kind enough to wake me up…!"

Levia giggled. "Don't mention it, Zipp," Levia calmed him down, "your body was doing some strange things, welcome back."

"I-I see…" he stood up and looked around, "why are you imprisoned here, Lady Levia…?"

She sighed and looked at the sealed serpent statue. "The priest imprisoned me here because he had the brilliant idea of ignoring my divinity and trying to take my partner away from me…"

"Fortunately I realized quickly and came here as soon as I could," I told the man named Zipp, "I'm just lucky those golden minnows lead me here--"

"Wait-wait-wait, WAIT!" Zipp cut me off, "while I was asleep I met a sweet Ancient, Hope was it…? Ya, she told me she's trying to guide the Loop in a different direction or something… then again, what is that Loop anyways…?"

SHAUNA LEE; CREATOR OF LIFE-

T wo months have passed in a flash. I kept being tested and checked by Sabrina, trained my fighting skills by Terry and was holed in my room studying for the theoretical and the method for the physical test. I couldn't sleep in my room without Terry, Anansi or Jay standing guard outside and around my room.

The day of the trial came and I was to face it without my guards who were reluctant to let me head in without them. "I'll be fine, everyone!" I tried to reassure them, "I trained for this moment for the last two months, I can defend myself after all."

Terry quietly gave me a firm hug and reluctantly released me. "Don't overexert yourself, aight?"

I nodded and headed inside.

The testing hall was grand, filled with many, many candidates and at the center was a giant ancient statue that had vibrant colors that haven't chipped. The statue was that of a beautiful and albino woman with ruby eyes and lips, long flowing and delicate silk dress and adorned with gorgeous and graceful jewelry.

Most of the candidates that filled the entrance hall were mostly actual children from the ages of twelve to fifteen. But some of the candidates that got approval from Behemoth to enter, though they were around the ages of twenty to thirty, were Sabrina's test subjects like me and prepared just as much as I had or more.

A booming intercom system told us to enter the halls of the written tests and all the candidates split into groups of others that they're familiar with, like families and childhood friends. While I tried to head inside I almost tripped over a lion cub's hind paw as he and his buddies snickered but I balanced myself in an instant but was the last to enter.

I sat in the far back and quietly skimmed through the pages that appeared from 'thin air', more like linked to one's soul so it's completely fit to the candidates' personal ideals and belief, testing their honesty and trust in themselves. While filling the pages with answers I remembered the studies I went through I was aware that the tests are to bring forth one's true ideals when they write them down with ink on paper.

Each test is usually planned ahead of the candidate's actual date of trial, so those tests can be set up by the families that have enough spiritual prowess or money, sometimes both to set their descendants for success.

Oddly enough I finished the very first as my test papers turned into a weapon for me to use in the test and had a ticket number seven attached to its handle and I headed down to the waiting room that was in a different room from the hall we were tested in. I've rightfully received many confused stares from the other candidates as they continued to focus on their own tests.

Two of my new teammates came in the room and began a small talk with me.

"I'm Kumo Iktomi," the arachnid kid introduced himself cheerfully, "nice to have another repeat testee here."

"Oh, I'm not a repeat…" I tried to clear it up, "but otherwise, I'm Shuana Lee, my pleasure."

"Whelp, I am repeating," a wolf kid told us, "my name is Shou LouGarou, pleasure is all mine."

While we were chatting away, the lion cub that tried to trip me during the entrance to the test zones came into the room. He had such an aura of pride but hatred towards us, his new teammates.

He tried to leave the room to ask the guards to change his teammates with his dear family members or even other mammals that aren't 'dogs'.

I stood up to introduce myself. "I'm Shauna Lee," I told him, extending my hand for a friendly shake, but He swatted me away with disgust and dusting his paw.

"Why would you act friendly with your enemy?" he curtly told me.

LouGarou barked at him, annoyed. "Unfortunately for us," he growled, "you *do* need to be a team player through this trial, understood?"

"I think I know what you mean…" I calmed Shou down, "you're an Aslan, aren't you?"

He grumpily looked away. "What gave that out?!" He glowered.

"Most Cats hate all Reptiles," I answered his question, ignoring the venom spilling through his words, "but I'm aware the Aslan family despises me most, so I can tell pure despise better than anyone."

The intercom buzzed, telling us to enter the trial grounds which are always an illusion of our worst nightmares and fears. Kumo, Shou and I walked ahead of the Aslan kid (who never introduced himself properly, mind you), but he was walking at our speed with an apprehensive look plastered all over his face.

"You okay there, Aslan?" I genuinely inquired.

"What's it to you, you slimy Reptile?" He retorted, visibly shaking.

I raised my arms in defense. "I'm not expecting you to be my friend right here right now," I hurriedly told him, "but having allies for support during the test *is* important.

"Why are you trying to ally yourself with your family's *enemy*," Kumo asked me, "he clearly despises you."

"*An enemy once an ally the next*," I quoted, "that's my motto."

"You're very strange…" Lou told me, "I've never heard such a motto before."

Kumo quietly pondered it. "Isn't it a saying by the Creator of Life…?" He mentioned.

I giggled. "I'm very inspired by them," I told them, avoiding saying the whole truth, "they're beyond my reach after all…"

Aslan snorted. "Damn straight Reptile," he pushed in, "only the Aslan clan has the real Creator as our leader."

"You mean Milla?" I said to directly.

"HOW FUCKING DARE YOU, REPTILE!" A familiar pissed tone followed through the winds. An image of the corrupted princess came to view with Cobra right next to her.

"What are you doing here, slut?" The image of Cobra told me, "you don't deserve any other life than being a brooding mare."

Kumo and Lou stared at my fears and I noticed that Aslan was shaking in his boots, staring at Milla's image.

"You're of the lower branch of the family, you bastard!" the image glared at the kid, "your only rightful place in the family is nothing more than a forgotten loser!"

I clenched my weapon.

"Whoa-whoa-whoa there, hoe!" The Cobra image bastard approached me, preparing to grab my naginata spear's edge.

"You're nothing but a bad memory of mine!" I said jabbing the weapon through it's hand, "I'm still carrying the guilt you caused me, but I won't waver!" I chopped off the illusion's hand.

"Kill that guy already!" Kumo cried.

It may sound easy to you, Iktomi. This guy's my worst nightmare.

A knife cut the skin on my arm. It was deep enough of a cut to make me bleed badly, but I was unable to close it. Kumo shook at the sight of my blood loss and began to cry uncontrollably.

"Iktomi, snap out of it!" Shou slapped the spider, "we gotta stop the bleeding!"

He took deep breaths, when he calmed down he spat out webs and began to stick the wound closed while looking below it while humming itsy bitsy spider and breathing shakily.

"Th-thank you, Kumo--" I stopped when he began to change and turned into a more human shape when his extra eyes became beady-like, his main eyes got bigger and his arachnid segmented arms turned into more of a human shape, similar to Anansi's. I smiled reassuringly at the successful spider boy and lost consciousness, hearing the Aslan cub shout my name in despair.

Who am I...? A Creator of a Menace..?

Why am I fighting? For my sake...?

Terry's...?

What do I want to achieve?

I want to help all of those who are suffering, but shouldn't I call for help myself...?

Everyone deserves happiness, but... am I?

Well...

I...

I should!

I have people that care for me, people that I trust and people that I love.

I want to make them proud!

That their help meant something, not just to me but to all people too.

I woke up in Terry's arms as he beamed at me with pride. "You're one amazing person, you know that?" he kissed my forehead with love and care, "all of your teammates passed the trial," a mirror was shove in front of my face, "and so did you."

I stared at the image in the mirror and barely recognised myself. My big scaly freckles were much smaller and delicate. I had a full set of teeth in my maw, my fangs were slightly bigger than those of a human but they were smaller than I was used to having. I raised my usually big, clunky and mostrous left arm with too much ease and realized it was the same human arm as my right hand, with small black claws for fingernails. Both my arms had the same type of freckles that I had on my face.

Terry set me back on my feet when I lost my balance thanks to the fact my normally bulky right leg was exactly the same length as the left and more human-shaped. I saw that the person that shoved the mirror to my face was an overly excited Anansi with Jay right next to him, trying to act cool.

"U-umm… Lady Shauna…?" the familiar voice of the Aslan cub came from behind me, "I don't know how to thank you enough."

I turned to look at him and saw that he had turned more human than the last time I saw him. I then put the pieces together and realized that I did help everyone pass.

"Don't mention it!" I tried to play it down, "at least your family won't kick you out, right?"

"Not quite," a different voice and a guy that looked late twenties to early thirties bowed to me, "little Joan and I are from the lesser branch of the Aslan family, which means that we never had a chance to be *seen* by the common folks and to be trained as assassins."

"I've never realized that," I voiced my concern. When I said that Joan and the ex-assassin stared at each other then at me and after that to Terry.

Terry chuckled. "Not surprised that you don't remember, Shaun," he said while getting stares from the two, "you awakened your true nature for the first time, after all."

"Meaning…?" the three of us asked him, bewildered.

Instead of explaining everything to us he dropped to one knee and popped the question I've never dreamt to have in my entire life.

"Will you marry me?" he asked me while holding my hand to his lips, "will you make our love official?"

I teared up while many candidates came in and out of the temple, staring at his proposal. "A-are you sure, Terry?" I asked him when he lifted his gaze to meet mine.

"Never been more sure in my entire existence," he answered me, with the most gentle smile I've ever seen him give anyone.

I nodded quietly and his smile widened to the warmest and loving smile I never thought I deserved and he hugged me.

"Lord Beast-Lord Beast!" Sabrina came running towards the temple where we still stood in front of, huffing and puffing, "we got an influx of people from a facility that was given to Miss Smith!"

"What?!" I asked her with urgency, "what's going on?!"

She hurriedly composed herself.

"I don't know myself, and Mr. Catwalk wouldn't tell me what's up…"

"Wait--" Terry stared at her, "you mean the weasel is here? With Lila's people?!"

"Well… yeah!" Sabrina hopped cheerfully but calmed down, "he did call for Ms. Lee for an update…"

Terry held my hand tightly. "Why?"

"I should probably head to him to get to understand the situation---" I was cut off by his absolutely terrified gaze, "why are you so worried? He is the head nurse that works with Lila…?"

"I'm coming with you," Terry declared, "and I ain't taking no for an answer."

Sabrina stared at him with confusion but shrugged and used some kind of wind magic and we arrived back at the lab. It was completely full with people from Lila's organization, human refugees included. I saw Russell hopping from kid to another before noticing us.

"Miss Shauna!" He looked at me approvingly, "I see you were successful with that trial thing, hard to recognize ya!"

Terry glared at him with absolute despise.

I ignored his glare and asked him bluntly- "what had happened for Lila to send those people away?"

Russell hushed me and guided me, with Terry following us to a back room. "Ms. Smith had been hacked," he told us with a grim look on his face, "Ms. Driscoll is fighting her off while sending not just these people, but everyone away for their safety."

"I need to help her!" I stressed to Terry.

He quietly gave me a small ring with an orb of clear emerald and sent me on my way with a peaceful smile.

OLIVER HARPER; CREATOR OF MATTER-

Suddenly Emile got a report from the park where my old (now resculpted) statue filled to the brim with refugees from Lila's organization- from 'ugly' folks and 'vile' humans in toe. Tenku and I flew in her stead in order to 'protect' her integrity that already got multiple hits, from her human friends getting support through the taxes paid by the 'valiant' proud folks and having a three way relationship with Tenku and I.

I approached the kids and not the guards and began to question them. "Why is everyone here?" I demanded. I did remember that this is par for the course right now… It's Lila's turn to perish, huh.

I noticed my mother, Marie Harper, plowing her way through the children, careful of hurting the now panicked people. "That golden DH woman sent us all here," she grumbled, "not telling us why we had to evacuate, or telling us why she would split everyone to those 'cities', or wherever we are."

"Oh, you are in a city," I informed her, "it's just the most obscure park in the city," I pointed to the statue, "but since the last vandalism, we had guards set here---"

"Ollie?!" My mother stared at the statue, "are you a war hero here?!"

Tenku stood in front of me in a defensive position. "Who is the lady, partner?" he asked me with apprehension, noticing the proud glow in my mother's eyes, "is she your mother, then?"

"Yes I am!" she grabbed Tenku's hand while beaming like a bright beacon, "by partner, don't ya mean- husband?"

Tenku blushed like a steamed lobster and tried to hide it behind his other sleeve. The guards tensed up as they saw how touchy feely my mother was but I gestured for them to stand down.

"About being a 'war hero' here- I'm basically a God here," I began answering her inquiries one by one, "not that I wanted to be, but Fate always has other ideas. For the husband part… we ain't officially married yet and the preparations will take quite a while--"

"I want a front line seat at the engagement, kiddo!" My mother declared.

I had to stop the conversation as I summoned my crwth.

"Leaving already…?" Tenku asked, puzzled, "we don't know why they're all here…"

I sighed while tuning my instrument. "They are here because Lila got hacked," I told him with a-matter-of-fact tone, "the Younger Twin- that Kaida woman- sent everyone away for their safety--"

"What for the name of God are ya talking about, kiddo?" Ms. Harper demanded, "speak like a normal soldier, will ya?"

"I can't right now," I told her, imagining the location and people I tried to reach, "but," I stared at Tenku while playing my crwth, "send what I just said as a report to Emile, she'll know what I meant."

I popped out to my wartorn home, the one that I usually lived in while being under Lila's commands. It was a simple ground floor one room apartment, where I stayed on my own while drinking myself senseless since the bar was right next to this room. I noticed that my lucky charm- a key fitting to the only analogic locked drawer with the needed the Hacking-Overdrive Gun that Lila makes during every loop (the previous ones that I have more awareness of) -including this one- in order to properly kill her brain to stop the cruelly puppeteered corpse.

This loop is clearly different than the previous ones, but for some reason, that part had not changed… Why does Lila have to die in order to protect the form of reality…? That's beyond me.

Deep in thought I went to sense Kaida's and Fish-Sticks auras but noticed it was much further away from each other but next to Kaida was… Shauna? How did she make it?! She's been during so many loops that had been cut short so, so, SO many times. If she's here… Maybe Lila will survive--

When I reached these two, Kaida was being treated by a different looking Shauna. They noticed me approaching with my clothes fluttering in a breeze. "Someone has been treated right," A quietly miffed fishy voice came to my ears.

"Dylan, when did ya get here?" Shauna asked him with surprise.

He put his hands on his waist with mild exasperation.

"Have you noticed our home is being raided, Miss Lee--" Fish-Sticks began to answer but was cut off by Tails.

"How did you even recognize me?" She demanded, "I barely recognize myself!"

"Let's focus on the task at hand," I said.

"Do you have the key?" Fish-Sticks asked me.

"So you remember the previous time now, are ya?" I mentioned, "and yes, I have it on me---"

"Why are you talking like you already know what this situation is?!" Tails continued, "Terry mentioned it too... What with this 'last time' shit?"

The three of us shared looks, having a staring competition for who'll answer her. I lost. "That is something you should clear up with Terry," I avoided her glare, "this is something you should've reached while being in his city."

"Fine-- I won't push it further," Shaun finally accepted that this situation is not a good place for those questions, "but what's the plan, since you lot already know what it is."

"Fish-Sticks and I will distract the humans and cyborg troops," I explained the plan, "Kaida will distract Lila's corpse while you will grab the gun that's locked with this key," I gave her the key, "it was my lucky charm while I had locked my memories away, don't lose it."

"Understood," Tails nodded and became camouflaged when we all steeled our resolve to be the most obnoxious distraction we can be.

The three of us took off and made the one possessing Lila to order a split of their troops. "So… Golden Dragon," the corpse said, "what are you bastards planning?"

Kaida chuckled confidently. "If I told you," she shot a light ball at the puppet, "it wouldn't be fun, huh Mr. Nightmare?"

"How did you get that idea, Kiddo?" It asked her cautiously.

"You remember what happened -Last Time- don't ya?" Kaida avoided the Raptor's tail and her extending claw.

"How…?" The corpse quieted down, "of course you'll be the one to remember, huh? Since your Elder can't remember enough to change the fate Lady Fate gave her many a time," It laughed loudly.

It went quiet.

I took off, taking as many flying soldiers as I can get and noticed someone that looked familiar. "Bud," I trapped the man in a quieting vortex, kicking his comrades off the air, "are ya a Kingstone by chance?"

He stopped and stared at me, utterly confused. "Why would you ask, Buzzer?" He asked me with his guard up but remained immobile. While we were having this small interaction all his comrades were down.

"For your interest," I continued, "your possible sister's no longer a human, if ya will," His jaw clenched, "not by any of our own hand, in case you wanna throw the blame at my feet."

"Then why would you tell me this, even if I am a Kingstone?" His guard was still up, "why would I be interested in that info?"

"I can tell you're concerned by this info, bud," I disarmed him and put down the wind barrier, "I'm not your enemy, aight?"

"Then why would you disarm me then?" He challenged me.

"The fact I don't want to be an enemy to you doesn't change the fact that you still see me as yours," I bluntly told him, "if not for anyone but my own safety," I gave him an acknowledging shrug.

He took a deep breath and took a bit of his guard down. "How do you mean she's a 'God'...?" The man finally asked me directly, "does it mean that she's alive but no longer a human...?"

"Pretty much," I answered, "I'm the same as her, a 'God', if ya will."

He looked around, seeing that all of his allies are down for the count.

Do you wanna help 'em?

A peppy and kind voice came from all around us and within our brains.

"Of course I wanna help my comrades!" He told the voice.

Do you believe they deserve a second chance in life?"

The voice continued, starting to come into view, slowly but surely.

"How do you mean, Ma'am?" He looked around, puzzled out of his mind, "by second chance, do ya mean..."

Letting them get a chance to live the lives they wanted.

It answered. A faint, young, golden skin dragon-looking girl came into view while smiling brightly. I could tell she wore a kimono looking overcoat laying over her shoulders but it was in contrast with her short sailor skirt and a loosely draped teal shirt. She had long, straight brown hair and piercing gold eyes.

She was still hazy but her personality was clear.

"Can you give them such a chance, Ma'am?" The soldier asked the girl.

"I want all of the people here to have a chance to change the destinies they were given at birth," she told us coming into a bit of clearer view, "I do have a soft spot for you kiddos, ya know?"

"Who are you?" I finally was able to string a word in.

She giggled playfully. "My name is Hope," she introduced herself, looking at Lila's husk. It began breathing again.

I prepared my crwth but she held her big arm to make not just me but Fish-sticks and Shauna halt. "What are you doing, Ms Hope?" I demanded, "the puppeteer hasn't left this body yet!--"

While we were set to fight the husk, the allies of Emile's older brother and another ally of his that was left conscious, had begun to fade away.

"Don't worry about them too much," she told the two, "you can say, that I'm resetting the lives they had until now--"

"Can you tell us why you aren't worried about Lila's corpse--" I was cut off by the eyes of the husk opening its eyes violently. It sat up straight and took a look at their hands and tried to stand up. Kaida rushed to it and helped it stand on its own.

"Kaida? What are ya doin'?" Gills asked her, confused.

"Elijah," she told the person inside the corpse, "it's you, aren't ya?"

"Ms. Driscoll?" It asked, "am I really in Lady Lila's body now?"

Kaida nodded with a comforting smile.

"Lady Hope?" Elijah looked at the golden chick, "thank you so much for giving me this chance!" She thanked Hope profusely.

Hope smiled kindly and cheerfully. "You're very welcome Little Star!"

The man who fought against Dylan just stared at Shauna intensely.

"What is it, buddy?" She finally demanded.

"You look exactly like my mother," he mumbled, "what's your name, kiddo?"

"Oh--" she smiled a stiff smile, "I'm Shauna Lee. What's yours?"

"I'm Jacob, Jacob Lee," he introduced himself, "pleasure to meet you."

Hope jumped up and down with agitation. "You two are family, ya know!" She strung them together, "you finally get to know each other and all you do is stare awkwardly at each other?"

She then walked over to Kaida and Elijah and patted Kaida's head.

"We're gonna change the deal you lot made with my sister," Hope told Kaida and Elijah, she turned to the Lee siblings, "you two should head back to dear Terry's domain, to catch up and---"

Shauna's eyes rolled to the back of her head and she began scratching herself, screaming in pain as if something is eating her from the inside.

"Wha-what's wrong, Shauna?" Jacob asked her, stumbling on his words, he looked at Hope with hope in his gaze, "what can I do for her?"

Hope took a deep breath while he picked up his tortured sister and cradled her in his arms. "I'll send both of ya to Beast's domain for her to start recovering," She put her hand on Shauna's forehead and it glowed gold, she put her hand down as Tails calmed down a bit, "this should do it for now. Terry will meet ya there, aight?"

The moment she said that a warm golden glow surrounded the two and they disappeared. Dylan stood there, staring at the fading glow.

"You… you were the one who helped me before, huh?" He challenged Hope, "weren't ya?"

She just gave him a confessious grin. "Ya got me, bud!"

DYLAN VANN; CREATOR OF STRATOSPHERE-

L et me make the last two months clear.

I have managed to get all, and I mean *ALL* of my past lives memories right in my brain. All intact, while I began beating the predatory priest and managed to keep both myself and everyone I care about.

Let's begin after I managed to get in contact with Roger and set up for the disturbing trio to knock them all out. We set up a trap and I was the bait, because, *obviously* I'm the prize for them to manipulate.

I headed to the central plaza, guns blazing but still having the robes of the rebellion on me. I ain't gonna be slutty just to look like prey. One of the Nightmare brothers noticed me and told his brother and doll.

They gave chase and I kept a safe distance between us, making a protective bubble tunnel to let them chase me without destroying the city.

"Wait there, Darling!" The pervert called for me, I stopped at an empty park, where I turned to him, playing the fearful prey act, "finally found you dear!" He swam to me and hugged me gently, "you must've been terrified of those bastards!"

I hugged him back and inaudibly stabbed him in his gut. Blood gushed out into the vacuum that I've created around the wound and when he realized the pain when he exploded blood from that wound. "If I was scared by anyone," I coldly glared at him, "it'll be *you*, bastard."

The Nightmares brothers grabbed for me and I dodged everything they tried to haul at me while their puppet was bleeding like fish in a bloody bowl mumbling 'why?'.

I pulled twin blades that I was given by Ara and danced around them, waiting for our set up to pull through. "Roger, NOW!" I shouted and golden beams of light shot up, burning the brothers.

"What with this light?!" Lust demanded, "MOTHER TAKE US HOME!"

They shouted in unison as they faded into shuttered-glass-like particles.

Roger came zipping down and took a look at the old priest losing pieces of himself alongside his blood. Tiamat rushed next to him and held his disintegrating hand while crystals slipped out of her eyes.

"I-I'm sorry, my love…" He apologized to her while fading away, "I've completely lost my mind there, went too deep with the desire of protecting those I love--" he coughed, "sorry for pushing you away like that," he shoved his arm to his chest and brought up a core of blue energy, "this belongs to you, Creator," Tiamat held it carefully, "I am aware of the loss of trust between us, but--" Levia came from behind me and took the orb from her hand and nodded, "That had been sealed by you two in order to help us control the husk, so the least I can do is take it out of my soul, huh?"

He faded away while his wife hugged him goodbye.

"Miss Tiamat…" Roger tried to comfort her.

"Call me Tia, okay son?" She smiled brightly, "I need to move forwards," Tia told him, "after all, that's what my late husband would've wanted of me while he was alive, right, Lady Levia?"

Levia smiled, set down that orb next to where she stood and hugged Tiamat. "He never really left you," she accidentally kicked the orb while comforting Tia and I got a wave of memories and emotions that knocked me out cold.

When I woke up in a different room and someone was curled around my body like an ivy. I patted the head that was on my chest and it perked up. It was Levia, blushing blue. She tried to sit up but I held her back to my chest.

"Were ya helping me while gluing yourself to me like this?" I asked while patting her head, "welp," I sat up and my stomach was growling like a thermal vent, "I could definitely use a nice meal with my dear partner," I caressed Levia's cheek with a smirk, "after all we've been through, right?"

Levia giggled. "So you remember everything now, huh?"

"Yup--" Roger came running into the room shouting with startled emergency, "what is it?"

"B-Boss!" He calmed down, catching his breath, "a lot of folks came to the location of our last fight," Roger took an even deeper breath, "they're all from Miss Lila's facility!"

And that's how I managed to remember every Cycle and realized what I had to do once more. Protecting everyone and getting prepared for the new Cycle to happen.

SHAUNA LEE; CREATOR OF LIFE-

Burning.

Poison

Acid.

Vomit.

Bile.

Pain.

Rage.

Guilt.

Fear.

Exhaustion.

Slumber.

…Up! Wake up-- Please--

The pain… It won't stop!

It won't stop!

It won't stop!

…I'm sorry-- I'm so sorry, Love--

It's all my fault--- I don't want to lose you again-- Again--- AGAIN!

Love… It's not your fault. It was never your fault. It always was inevitable, after all- it was decided at my inception by Fate herself? I'll always live and die for your sake, right?

WAKE UP! I'm begging from all the Ancients, PLEASE--

I finally found the light at the end of this torturous cave that is fille with pain and sufferings. In front of the light stood a small statured woman, with pale hair, eyes and skin dressed with a thin and silky white nightgown. She looked like a smaller but older version of myself. Was she my mother…? I've never seen her image before, so I can't say for sure.

The small woman blocked the path towards the light. "Are ya sure you want to progress through the door?" The pale woman inquired, "do you want Fate to win once more?"

"Who are you, Ma'am?" I countered, "why would you even ask this question?"

The ghost chuckled and began to change. She grew in height and had turned gold colored skin, dark brown and sparkling golden hair. Her eyes turned pure blue like bright aquamarine. She wore a cloak made of golden gilded stork feathers, underneath she wore a simple white linen shirt with ankle length grave keeper boots. "Sharp as ever I see, Sis," She answered my confused stare, "But I should introduce myself to you once more," She held my hand with her oddly frozen hands, "my name is Jin, the Golden Reaper."

"Wai-WAIT! What do ya mean by 'Reaper'...?" I frantically demanded, "like-- Am I dead---?"

She calmly shook her head. "Not yet, Sister, not yet," Jin bore into my eyes, "but it is up to ya, this time at least," I just blankly stared at her, the Golden Reaper stumbled over her words and laughed while trying hard to explaining, "What I mean is," she gestured to the door behind her, "This what people usually call 'the Door to Heaven', or as I call it- 'the Other Side', where all mortals are judged, but mortal gods like you are sent to a new life instantly."

"But why can I have a choice *this* time?" I pondered.

"Because my master gave it to you," Jin answered me with a matter-of-fact tone, "Lady hope decreed me to give you a chance once per a life, ya see."

Realization set in. "That strange woman is your master?" I demanded, "I do see why, however."

"There's harsh," the Reaper snickered, "but what will ya choose?"

I took a deep breath. "If I get this chance to return to the life I know," I fixed my eyes on hers, "I'll take it."

Jin took my hand and led me back into the darkness I just faced moments ago. She turned the top of her scythe into a brightly burning lantern and guided me through the sufferings of each life, absorbing and facing each pain head on. I realized that every time I died I caused so much pain to those sakes I had died for.

"Death is a blessing to those who passed the First Gate," the Golden reaper pointed out to me, "but a curse to those who live on."

I saw images of the many versions of Behemoth crying at my many dead versions. He kept locking his emotions each time, even though he kept moving onwards, always hoping for my return, reincarnating and going through the same pain and guilt time and time again.

"And the worse curse for those who outlive their loved ones," Jin slammed her lantern staff on the ground, "is remembering both."

I woke up with a warm blanket hug. I realized I wasn't in my usual designated room before marital unity. I was in Terry's room, within his arms and he was shirtless. My heart began pumping hard when he noticed my heartbeat and raised his head in surprise and relief.

"Sh-Shauna?" He sat up and tried to fix his bedhead, "h-how are you doing?" Terry stumbled on his words with his clear concern.

I looked up, my heart beat like a mad-horse and took deep breaths. "I'm sorry for worrying you so much, Love," I answered his concerns with a quick hug, "but thank you for always waiting for me," I smiled brightly.

Tears rolled down his cheeks when he embraced me back, shaking wildly. "I've waited for so damn long," he kissed my forehead gently, "I was told by everyone to stop waiting for you, to stop loving you…"

"But you've never listened, huh?" I playfully snickered.

Terry laughed a relieved and deafening laugh. "Damn straight, Love," he kissed me all over, "I'm so happy!"

"Pops?!" Anansi came running in with obvious worry in his eyes, but when he saw why he had such a reaction he ran out of the room for a few moments and returned with Jay and my brother.

Jay stared at me and tearfully smiled in desperation. "Finally!" He jumped in bed and bear-hugged us, "I've already lost all hope!"

Anansi joined in and pulled my brother in the hug as well.

"I-I can't breath!" I choked out and was finally released from the clutch of love, "I've lost hope myself, if I'm being honest."

"So… sis," Jacob sat cautiously next to me, "do you wanna be a family?"

I giggled. "I'd love to be one, brother--" he hugged me.

"I have lost all hope of having a family," he told me when he released me from his arms, "I applied to the Eastern republic out of spite to father and just resigned to Death's Door."

I solemnly smiled. "Will you believe me if I said I met a Grim Reaper right next to that place?"

"Well," My brother began talking but was cut off by a screeching of Russell and Sabrina running in with absolute glee.

"We've heard the news!" Sabrina ran in and tackle-hugged me.

"Both news, Missy," Russell looked different. He seemed to have passed the trial as well, "You're gettin' hitched, huh?"

A few months afterwards we had the best wedding any small child would dream about, but it was calmer, sweeter and supportive from everyone. I wore a simple gold embroidered white gown, no jewels or finery and felt as pretty as I always dreamt of being. Terry wore a simple tuxedo with green handkerchief in the pocket and holding a small jade box when he initiated the vows.

"How does a god marry another?" Terry began, "once for all of existence, twice for a bond and thrice for love. I'll never forget the first time we created the world and all of those we love. I never had gotten the chance to choose a life with my partner before then, and now I have been given a chance to finally do it once more, thanks to our loving Mother and her powers of finally changing one's Fate decreed destiny," He opened the box and pulled a whole emerald ring and slid it to my finger, I pulled my red carnelian matching box and slid a solid matching ruby onto his and he took off the vail and gently kissed me.

"A god who had waited many times and many lives," I returned, "never lost their hope and love, only to be bound for a life of hope and joy, love and trust. Who have been cursed for a life of loss and burden and finally were blessed by those who lived and gone for a bond to crushing for one," I entwined my fingers in his, "but lighter combined."

When the celebrations calmed down we went to Terry's room to consummate the unity. When we finished I got a message from Kaida and Elijah to come back with everyone they sent over to Beast to the settlement. I reluctantly told my darling partner that I had to go and he nodded in understanding.

"Make me proud," he told me, holding my face tenderly as I went to the refugee camp to inform everyone that they were going home. Quite a few locals hopped on the wagon as well, wanting to check what the Golden Twins have created.

OLIVER HARPER; CREATOR OF MATTER-

The last few months became a blur of cleaning, organizing, fixing and repeating. Dylan, Michael and I took one area. Kaida, Elijah and Hope to another. We built new homes and facilities like medical centers where different types of doctors would come from all over the world, including humans. Other facilities included an indoor market place with stalls and stands to give to anyone who wanted to buy and sell unique goods, multiple small pools and an electrical walkway for ease of walking around and expending less energy.

Mike was huffing and puffing after a while of building a house. "Are we authorized to build stuff like this?" He asked with an exhausted and trembling tone, he sighed and fell flat on the ground, "it's much easier to break stuff than building it up," he snickered, "but why won't we get help from more professional people?"

I picked up the tarp that fell over him and gave him a cup of cold water. "Ms Kaida told us we will make it a surprise to everyone," I sat next to him, "and we do have thorough plans that were given by, much far, more capable person we could ask for--"

"You mean Ms Elijah?" He answered with a question, "I don't get how she's now within Ms Lila, but I ain't gonna question it."

"Oh, taking a break now don't cha?" Hope came from the area the three ladies dominated, "I guess everyone needs a break from time to time, huh?"

Michael started to stutter his inquiries. "U-umm… Ms Hope?" he shook with clear fear, "y-you're a God, right?" Hope nodded with wide eyes, "then why are you interfering now? Don't Gods usually stay away from us lowly mortals?"

She sat up, crossing arms and legs with playful annoyance. "I already told yall why I interfere right now," The Golden Goddess pouted, "I have a really soft spot for all mortals, I'll have ya know."

"Wh-what I meant with my question is to... why do you feel any sort of connection with us mortals?" Michael bluntly but cautiously asked, "You wield so much power as a God, and I'm sorry that I've never heard of you before and--"

Hope stopped his stumbling with a gleeful laughter. "I may be a God," she playfully grinned, "but I'm not big for being known and respected as a higher being," she drew in the sand with her big finger, "humans to me are children that have outgrown my original planning," the drawings came to life and played around, "but there is a reason for the loop this world is bound for," she flicked the sand creations and drew more, "because my beloved children should know where to stop with playing Gods with their own."

"Do you mean like the Eden Program?" Mike mentioned, "I've never looked into it so I don't know much about it if anything."

"You're very knowledgeable for a field soldier," I called him out.

"Well... I wanted to be more aware of why we were sent here," He answered me, "Jacob memorized more from it but I don't know more than its codename..."

"Then lemme tell you what it means to the future, or lack thereof, of humanity's freedom," Hope cut me before I was about to tell him off, "the Eden Program is something that all of the 'warring' but actually united empires that 'fight' each other in order to keep making money, scientific progression and keeping their populace always afraid but extremely content at the same time,"

She noticed our confused stares and playfully snickered, "do you really think that the Eastern Republic would come to hack Lila without the help of the Western Unity or even the Southern Empire in order to grab her repeatedly updated antivirus systems that come from them in the first place," the Golden Goddess sighed,

"But hybrids and soldiers like you are always rallied to fight, trained to kill and never question your positions -like- ever... I don't want humanity to stagnate, but I don't want you to lose the freedom through the Eden Program which researches into the Gate of the Lands of Eden, which is a domain humans should not access unless most of the Ancients approve such entry," she crushed all of the sand images and sent them into a breeze, "if they force it, their freedoms will be stripped away and all my work would be for all for naught."

"I've never realized that," Mike finally spoke up, "it always was hidden in such obvious places in the world we live in…"

"I've never known it myself," I admitted, "I always believed that everyone was everyone's enemy, including Gods like us."

"I doubt that Emile knows that either, being completely honest," Dylan came by and grabbed a cup from the bottle Hope set next to her, "I wasn't aware of it myself but we can damn well ask 'em."

"Don't doubt them," Hope scolded him, "some of that knowledge was just safer with one of the partners than both," she sighed, "you usually never remember that truth when you lot reincarnate so I understand why you have such doubts right now."

"What do you mean by 'reincarnating' and all of that?" Michael scratched his clueless head, "but never mind that-- that Eden Program sounds like a bad time, what should we do?!"

"Once we are finished with our rebuilding we'll start the planning of our offense proposal, aight?" Hope stood up and dusted off the dirt, then walked away.

After a few hours we were done with the homes and facilities, Micheal, Gills and I were doing basic cleaning and maintenance when Hope approached us again.

"The two of ya are to head back to your partners and guide all the kids and families back here," she sternly told us.

Mike stared at her in bewilderment. "My partner is with his sister--"

"Did I stutter?" her eyes went wide as wide yellow saucers, "you'll meet your sister and teammates soon enough."

I headed back to the park and Tenku told me what had happened while I was fighting that Nightmare thing. He made sure that everyone was taken care of with as much respect as possible, with warm tents, sleeping bags, food, the works. People from all over the capital came and directly donated stuff to the impoverished Bird Hybrids. I was also told that the Itachi Catwalk research has been completed and many of the kids here passed their ceremonies and became more human looking.

"Everyone of yall will have to make a choice, including the nice visitors here," I projected my voice, "you can come with me to the New Golden Settlement that Fish-Sticks, Ziz's brother, Ms Kaida, Ms Elijah and Lady Hope built an appropriate new town to welcome anyone who wants to live there."

Quite a few familiar hands were raised alongside some new ones, including Tenku. I then guided everyone who raised their hand to the new town we rebuilt.

Dylan Vann; Creator of Stratosphere-

When I told that everyone could come back home, a mostly fishy girl told me she didn't want to go home, a failure that can't go on land. Most of the excited guys that were preparing to head back turned mostly human bodies, are those that wanted to stay the are the ones' similar to the girls' situation.

The girl's name was Rosa. She's a pink skinned young 24 years old woman. She was raised at the Southern Empire and was deemed a failure due to the fact that she was weak bodied and unable to live anywhere without a water bubble right in her gills.

When the base was raided she was left for dead and Raptor herself picked her up herself and built her a regenerating water bubble so she could experience land like everyone else, through some incredible design based on John Arbeider's design.

A beautiful woman determinedly approached us. She was dressed with opulent and marvelous layered garbs of gold, aquamarine and coral fabrics and on her back she has wing-like vibrant coral reefs. Folks from around us mentioned that it has been forever since Lady Otohime came to town, let alone show interest in anyone outside her kin.

"Young Ms." Otohime regally addressed Rosa, "are you young Rosa perchance?" Rosa looked completely baffled by the Lady's Greeting.

"Umm… who are you, Ma'am?" Rosa challenged her back.

Otohime waved her garbs with annoyed dignity. "I'm Lady Otohime for you, young lady," she finally properly introduced herself, "I'm the Queen of the Dragon-Merfolks," the Lady proudly declared, "and you, my child, have the potential I have been looking for in centuries."

"Wh-what?!" Rosa demanded in surprise, "what kind of potential?"

"To become my successor, child," Otohime answered her as a matter of of calm fact, "you're but a hatchling that just needs some proper training---"

"WAIT-WAIT-WAIT-Wait, wait, Ma'am?" The pink fish stopped her speal, getting annoyed stares from the locals, "why me, though?"

"You're a different breed of sea-folk, child," Otohime's wings fluttered, sending off fish and algae around her, "a Dragon-Mer like all my kin," she saw Rosa's completely baffled face and elegantly snickered, "you also bare the same mark as I," she took off a part of her clavicle and a golden glowing birthmark shown, "the Mark of Hope."

"None of your subordinates can take the mantle?" I interjected.

Otohime glared at me with regal disapproval. "None of my kin bear such a concentrated amount of Lady Hope's mark," she answered me curtly, "those with such a mark always advance society, whether they are aware of it or naught, they prevent reality's stagnation. That's why Rosa is the future of my people."

"Pretty great reasoning, kiddo," an unfamiliar man's voice joined our conversation, "Little Rosa here has more potential than you, O' Majestic Majesty." The man cackled.

A man with marble pale skin, fiery red hair and blood red eyes that has a dark slint within them, glowing silver. He was dressed like a simple idol type of guy, a maroon polo shirt under black leather jacket that had quite a few pins embedded in it. He wore dark skinny jeans and some simple sneakers. He looked no older than early twenties but by the way he talked like an old-ass man.

"And who, pray tell, are you young man?" Otohime demanded.

The man chuckled, as if enjoying this scrutiny. "I'm Obsidian Nightclaw, pleasure meeting ya," He playfully introduced himself, "also known as the Ancient of Malice."

Otohime stared at the man in bewilderment. "YOU'RE Lord Malice?!"

She stumbled on her words a bit, quite terrified of Obsidian, "I-I've never thought you'd be… like that."

Obsidian gave her a death glare. "Don't EVER call me Malice, understand?" He stated coldly, then smiled gently as if nothing had happened, "please, call me Obsidian or Obi or any of these derivatives."

"You are quite different than how I imagined you'll be like that," Otohime stared at him in pure confusion, "You ARE an Ancient, correct?"

"Then you haven't actually met Hope, I'll presume," I joined it to break the tension while Obsidian howled in laughter, "she speaks more common than a country bumpkin."

Obsidian rubbed his eyes as if they were a bit itchy. "Sounds about right," The fiery man affirmed, "that's what made me fall in love with her," he turned quiet for a few moments then faced Roger, "I wondered… how did you manage to completely purify those two Lords?"

Roger clammed up but when he saw a kind smile from Malice's face he calmed down a little. But just a little. "A-are ya upset with it, Mr. Obsidian?" He began to try to apologize profusely.

Obsidian stopped the tirade with a playful smile. "Don't apologize, buddy," the fiery man reassured the boiling fish, "I'm more curious than 'upset'."

"U-umm… Mr. Obi?" Rosa gawked at Obsidian, "what's the real reason yer here, really?"

Obsidian burst into a lighthearted laughter. "Very perceptive of ya, kiddo," he tried to avoid answering her clearly, "but I can't tell ya just yet, aight?"

Otohime became incredibly anxious and wobbly. "Child," she said with a nervous urgency, "come with me right away--"

Obsidian smiled a comforting smile and pat Rosa's head gently. "You are a young Dragon-Mer with no actual experience with your own natural ability," he affirmed Otohime with a confirming nod, "you can only grow from now, to train with people that have the wisdom you deserve,

There has always been a system that needed some sort of human sacrifice, but since humans stopped falling and surviving long enough for the morph to happen. You, Rosa, are the future of the Guardians of Creation, the Dragon-Mers' future lies with you."

"You are the Ancient of Malice, correct?" Obsidian nodded in confirmation to Otohime's confusion, "why would you care for my kin and about our mission?"

The fiery man took his hand off Rosa's head and crossed his arms in defiance. "The reason I care for all mortals and the other folk is due to the fact that my partner, Hope, cares for you," he answered her honestly, "but I also treasure their fleeting existence on its own right, even without Hope's love for all mortals. I always was enthralled by them, despite my origins, understood?"

Lady Otohime calmed down quite a bit and gave a small sigh. "How noble of you, Lord Obsidian," she respectfully bowed to him, fish and algae got agitated again buzzing around her, "thank you for your support, my Lord."

She opened a portal of bubbles and led Rosa through it while she looked back at Obsidian that was waving her farewell.

When the two were gone Roger became ecstatic and extremely excited. "Mr. Obi, Mr. Obi," he zipped around him, "do you want to see the machine we used, right?" Roger bolted around and then to the direction of it, "I got this amazing stroke of genius and got my hand on that awesome material--" He dragged Obsidian away.

"I'll be taking everyone back," I told them as they inched away from the park.

OBSIDIAN GHOSTBANE; ANCIENT OF MALICE-

I was swimming along with the young man that was working as Ciel's right-hand man, Roger Sun, as I was briefed before coming here. We swam to the location where those kids were purified and swam up to the purifying machine, opened it up and there was Hope's crystallized blood as its main component for purification.

"Is it possible to crystallize blood to begin with…?" Roger stared at the crystal when I explained, "if so… isn't it a precious material then?"

I scratched my ear, as if to show that I have no idea. Which I truly don't. I chuckled instead. "Whelp," I avoided answering the puzzled boy, "you shouldn't wave around a powerful material like that to begin with."

Roger straightened up like a rod. "Mr. Obi, sir!" He got right into dismantling the machine and taking the blood crystal carefully and tried to give it to me. I looked at the gem, then to his apologetic face and back at the gem then repeated this quietly for a bit, "wouldn't be safe with ya, sir?"

I cracked up laughing and he stared at me, confuzed. "It was given to you, bud," I calmed down and shoved the hand carrying the crystal back to him, and shook my head, "you should keep it, aight?"

He put it in the box Hope gave it to him in and then into his backpack. A spark of realization shone in his eyes. "I know that the things you told that giant Lady and this Rosa girl of your reasons for helping 'em, but what I still don't get is… why?"

"No need to be confused 'bout that, kiddo," I plainly answered, "if you really want me to talk your ear off, say so!"

He nodded furiously. "If by telling me your story will make me understand you better, sir, I'm a real great listener!"

I stifled a chuckle then cleared my throat. "Fine," I relented, "but make sure you don't mix in your human morals into it, aight?" He nodded excitedly then stopped, took a seat and looked up at me curiosity shining in his eyes.

"As you've heard from dear Otohime, I'm the Ancient of Malice, darkness and corruption itself," Roj tilted his head in visible confusion, "hard to believe that a being at myself would try and protect creation, isn't it?" He nodded in agreement, "that was thanks to a Fate decreed plan gone incredibly wrong-

"A long-long-LONG time ago, before time itself two beings came to exist- the depths of darkness and despair, Abyss and myself, a being with a contradictory nature to the domain I govern. We then created our own version of life forms, our children, the Nightmare kind never knew anything else but the darkness in which we lived, in order to continue the peaceful darkness and fill our lonely lives.

"Then two more beings came to exist and took the first forms of creation- Lord of Space and it's corridors, Labyrth, and the Lady Who Waits for No-One, Creator of Time, Chrona and they came to create their own creations- their eldest child, the Lady of Rules and Stability, Miss Fate, or Destiny; The middle child, The Lady of Understanding and Progression, Lady Knowledge-

"Through the flow of time creations and other beings that came out of nowhere themselves took root and settled over the newly created Realm of Many, created by Chrona and Labyrth-

"Once the root of divine and mortal lives brought forth an abnormality that made Chrona give birth to a seemingly odd creation- that would be Hope, a being that was accidentally conceived and brought forth her own brand of chaos and jealousy from her eldest sister, Fate. She then created a destiny so gruesome that the chaos Hope brought to the world would be stabilized and prevented.

"Once the Ancient child reaches the age of 500 mortal cycles~

She would perish by the hands of Malice themselves~

At the garden of Heaven Lilies is to be washed with a~

rain of her purifying blood~

"In this fate I was written down as a force of good, which was odd for me at the time due to not knowing of the fires of jealousy burned in both and brought them together a bond shared by Fate and Abyss shared hatred towards the same girl, Hope.

"I didn't even know why I was destined to to a thing that was supposed to be beneficial to creation by time and space so I vowed to never pull through with such selfish destiny force on me by Fate. Abyss punished me for even speaking that piece of mind each time with so much searing and lashing I lost all my pain sensation to basically everything- from direct fire to huge gashes that end up with an immense blood loss.

"Once five hundred mortal cycles were done I reluctantly went and tried to be over with but dear little Hope was at the destined place and when she noticed me she introduced herself with a smile the thawed my frozen heart a little bit and I decided to teach her how to fight instead, so no one else would harm her, me included.

"Every time I was meant to kill Hope we would just hang out and check up on her progress in training and talking about her newest creations, from animal looking folks to hairless apes in their many versions. We also talked about the way Destiny, or Daisy as Hope calls her, belittles and judges everything she does and creates.

"Once Hope reached adulthood she was more assertive towards the desire of breaking both our fates- mine to be always bound to darkness and loneliness with a fate of destruction, and hers to be a catalyst for chaos and imbalance, to die by my hands. She gave me a piece of herself, similar to what she gave ya, and that planted the seed I needed to break my own cycle.

"After we were discovered Fate made a deal with Hope- if she proves to Destiny that she's not a force to be feared, Hope came with a solution- becoming mortal herself and subjecting herself to the laws placed upon mortals by Fate to prove a base of trust and confidence.

"Once their bet was up all of those who were fond of the memories of her existence as a powerful Ancient, as a being of light but chaos as well. I was to return to Lady Abyss's side since I had practically no memories of our first meeting in past life. But I was never going back to her and decided to fall for mortal Hope and keep an unknown love for her, even though I wasn't 'supposed to.

"After centuries passed, the creation of the multiverses due to Hope's will to free humanity from the bounds of all gods in the Realm of Many and breaking her own soul in the process into many versions of herself, who have their own soul alongside her dominance.

"As ya can tell, she finally succeeded in her bet and decided to interfere in worlds that need such direct intervention~

"This is an incredibly abridged story of my reasoning to help Hope protect the reality she created," I summarized and I was surprised by the very awake and full of understanding face staring back at me.

"I want to help more than anything!" Roj finally spoke after realizing how quiet I've become, "I want you to train me!"

I smiled reassuringly and nodded. "I'm willing but," I warned him, "it'll take 'bout five years for me to be done with ya."

He looked panicked and started calculating. "Do we even have the time-_"

I stopped him and shook my head. "Put your trust in me, aight?"

Roger nodded in acceptance and we headed to a portal I created.

HOPE ANGELBANE: THE GIVER OF CHOICE

We arrived at the location Obi told us to come to in five days. The place is the back of the main summit building in the center of No-Man's-Land for a peace talk with the five of us and the human leaders of the Big Three and the leading scientists of the E.D.E.N. program. We want to prevent the breach of the Land of Eden to keep humanity safe. That was what I was planning to say, but I just have a knack to take things off track.

"So… we need to wait for someone to open this door for us, right?" Oliver asked, puzzled, "who's gonna open it and how? Doesn't it complicate things for the guy inside?"

The door opened up to two heroes that Obsidian trained himself.

"Who's the chick with ya, Roger?" Dylan asked, not surprised by the look of an oddly older more human Roj.

"When did you get the time to age up?" Oliver demanded, "it's been only five days!"

Roger busted out laughing. "Did you not hear how long I've actually been away, huh?" He started to calm down with deep breaths, "Lara, wouldn't you be a dear and introduce yourself to the gang?"

"M-my name is Clara Vann," she bowed to us respectfully, "glad to finally meet you all, especially you, cousin!"

Dylan looked from Roger to Clara, very baffled. "I still have some biological family," he stared at Clara, clearly apologetic, "but I have no recollection of ye."

Lara seemed to deflate. "You should be aware that, somewhere, there are other people who are blood related and care for you," She spoke empathetically, "and your biological uncle that wanted to get ya out and a cousin who admires you like a hero!"

Dylan looked flabberghasted. "I'm no hero, cuz," he told her, without empathy, "I'm a person who killed your family after all."

She grabbed his hand and pulled his face close to her face and stared him down. "My father knew the danger of releasing you," she hissed, "and I knew as much as well, so don't go losing emotions on me," Clara released his arm as he straightened up with a broken look on his face, "YOU are my hero, don't lemme down, okay?"

I put my hand on his shoulder blade and rubbed it for a bit. He turned around and hid behind a boulder nearby to cry. Clara realized and ran to him and after a bit of consultation he came back with puffy eyes and a runny nose which was rubbed off on his jacket sleeve.

"You okay there Boss?" Roger worriedly asked.

Dylan took a deep breath. "Yeah," he confirmed, "I ain't breaking down in the meeting if yer concerned."

"I'm glad that you somewhat released your pain for now, Ciel," I told him, using the name I first gave him when I created him, "we'll need your cool head inside."

Dylan burst into laughter. "Haven't heard that name since you gave my life," he seemed to cheer up a bit, "thanks Hope, I needed that."

"Let's get going everyone!" Roger exclaimed and led us inside, closing the door behind us, "I'll try and be brief- Obi made sure that everyone who's who is in there so don't do anything reckless," he glanced at Oliver, "understood?"

Ollie became huffy and screeched: "why would you only glare at me you prick?!" he demanded, "I'm not an idiotic, ballsy and impulsive I was a year ago!"

"Really, Keir?" Shauna giggled, both at the mention of the name I gave him and the knockout she was about to dish, "you've always been the most impulsive guy I know."

Kaida cleared her throat. "We're getting closer to the summit room," she scolded the two, "we need to be presentable."

"Are you…?" Clara stared unashamedly at the mostly nude Kaida.

I giggled, then took off my overcoat and helped her dress up. "Humans are strange like that," I told her, "and ya can keep it, as a mark of my stead."

Kaida tied her new dress and looked to the door as it opened up.

KAIDA DRISCOLL: THE GOLDEN GODDESS

Once I donned the mantle of being Sister Hope's stand in for this meeting was a great honor that I trained hard to deserve. I felt ready to take my place as a somewhat new God. Aiden Blake was guarding the door as Lord Obsidian, who organized this entire meeting like a Boss, announced our coming into the room.

"Let us welcome our new guests with No Hostility, *understood*?" he glared at all the residents who gestured for their reluctant guards away, "now, shall we introduce ourselves?"

A middle aged man introduced himself as the Prime Minister of the Eastern Republic. His name was Richard Kingstone. Oliver chirped when he heard that.

"Why would you be so rude as to interrupt me?" the Prime Minister demanded.

Keir stifled a laugh. "I apologize for my indiscretion," Ollie started up, "but, perchance, are you looking for an Amalia Kingstone?"

Richard bulging eyes looking surprised but was cut off by Emperor Albert Fearor, the new Emperor of the Southern Empire who went off laughing. "The apparent living God here seems omniscient," he cleared his throat, "but you clearly wear your unnecessary objective on your sleeve.

An older woman, who interjected to introduce herself as the President of the Western Unity, Scarlet Lee, sighed with peev. "You clearly haven't read the summary of her latest search two months ago…" she mentioned appalled, "she was confirmed of having become the Goddess Ziz, who was captured accidentally five years ago, by your own nation might I add."

"But that was some odd bird girl that released the friends of Aamlia who we were questioning," Dick said, enraged, "we could not confirm who she was at the ti--"

Obsidian Interjected. "Oh, you poor summer child," He chuckled, "you would deny who the girl really was for the rest of any meeting, correct?"

Richard glared at the Ancient. "She was a human purist activist!" The Minister continued with his denial, "she would never have stooped to the level of gene therapy like all of you!"

Obi shrugged. "Deny it till you die, why don'tcha?" He gestured to the last person in the session, "now, shall *you* introduce yourself, Catalyst?"

"I am no Catalyst but," she bowed to us in clear curiosity and delight, "my name is Hanna Sun, the head of the E.D.E.N. Program which is run by the kind benefactors here," she gestured to the residents on the table including Obsidian but trembled when she did.

Obsidian roared in laughter and took a deep breath and gestured for us to begin.

The Creator trio introduced themselves one after the other and Sister Hope gestured for me to go before her. "I am Kaida Driscoll, once known as Dragon Hybrid No.56, under the Western Unity's watch and the successor of the Goddess Eurynome," they listened quietly and I began to get nervous but Hope was right next to me, reassuring, "and I want you to understand why the Rapture Procedure of the E.D.E.N. Program should not be launched."

"WHAT?! WHY?!" Hanna demended, "because we will achieve Godhood like you?!"

"You know that's not what she meant," Roger hissed, "you don't know what'll happen, you Snake!"

"Roger Sun, you have little to no voice in this meeting!" Hanna hissed back.

Scarlet slammed her hands on the meeting desk, silencing the hissing snake pit. "Do *you* know what happens once we achieve this, little Goddess?" She demanded of me.

I nodded with stern confidence. "Certainly," I spoke with poise and the four residents stared in awe and bewilderment, "If the Rapture Procedure will come to fruition, humanity's freedom will be revoked--"

"Right-right, AS IF!" Hanna cackled, "do you really think we'll believe some new God that thinks so highly of herself--"

Hope zapped through the air and slammed her hand on the researcher's chest sending her flying off her feet and slammed to the wall. While the human residents were alarmed, we were not. "Let me introduce myself," she grabbed the now morphing Hanna, "My name is Hope Angelbane," the woman's hair changed and rose up with sparks of a starting lighter, "and I am the one who bet my Godhood for the sake of humanity," She released the now burning hair and completely different face and demeanor Hanna to the ground.

"WH-WHAT IS SHE?!" Kingstone freaked out, "WHAT'S GOING ON?!"

Scarlet quickly regained her composure. "Clearly she didn't have our interest in mind, did she?" The President placed her hand on the Minister's shoulder and patted it repeatedly, "You're new to these kinds of situations aren't you, sir?"

The flaming woman got up, enraged with her hair burning brighter. "Hope, you inexcusable bitch!" She screeched with the area around her melting and burning, "you are *not* to interfere!"

Hope chuckled. "If I didn't intervene, Fie," she summoned a shield to protect the human and hybrid nations' leaders and ushered them away, "you wouldn't get your own chance to meddle this far, wouldn't ya think?"

The flaming woman, Fie, calmed down eerily and snapped her fingers. "You're too late, dear Hope-less bitch!" She smirked with prideful confidence, "the Rapture has begun!"

"Take the human leaders to safety!" Hope calmly commanded Cherith, Keir and Ciel who rushed the three leaders and their guards away from the building with summoned portals to their domains when the three of us headed down to the Rapture Program Core.

We rushed faster than Time would've allowed and reached the core and we saw a portal opening to the Land of Eden, but it didn't get far before Hope stretched her hand. "Mother Time I Wish for Your Help in Order to Stop Humanity's Despair," she called her spell, "Reach to the Depths O' Space to Alter the Forms O' my Domain Above."

The opening of the rapture slowed down and suddenly opened to another location, as she turned her hand in an anti-clockwork direction which turned back the opening to begin with. "Obi, do be a dear," she told Lord Obsidian as she began to show strain.

Obi nodded and faded in and out shapes and shadows and the machine shattered to pieces.

"I will not let you stop Lady Abyss's desires!" Fie came sparkling in and forcing Shapeless Nightmares to rebuild the machine, "why would any of you trust humanity with choice?!"

"Children," Obsidian used a dark and demanding tone, "you are not to obey the Catalyst, UNDERSTOOD?!" Most of the Shapeless scurried to the shadows but quite a few remained.

Hope went out like a light due to exhaustion as the remaining Shapeless started to slowly multiply, building the machine and crawling their way all over Hope's body while Obsidian was enraged.

I crumpled to the ground and was at a loss of what to do.

Then a spark came from above and the Creation Trio came waltzing in with music, grunting and slushing. Their prowess lit up hope in my heart.

"Lucky we came back in time, ey?" Keir was killing it with music out of his crwth.

"Hope really shouldn't astral project in the middle of a fight!" Cherith came in and slashing her spiritual hammer, slamming all the Shapeless off of her, "but I do understand why she did. Though."

"Agreed," said Ciel, freezing the water in the air, stunning the building Shapeless solid then they faded back to the abyss, Dylan swiped his forehead of sweat, "Our newly made Goddess needs to learn a bit more, however."

I was stunned. Fie approached me with blades at the ready. She began swiping away, I was cut the first time, realizing that shit hit the fan and I got ahead and dodged harder for my life.

"It is true, you damned little hatchling!" She taunted me with a maniacal grin plastered on her face, "You do not deserve being a God, much less a stand in for an Ancient!"

It began getting to me.

"Stop that you Burning Catalyst!" Aiden stood in front of me, taking the brunt of her last slash, "YOU don't have your own agency other than being one after all!"

Fie's fires burned blue and she landed a direct hit on Aiden.

"NOOOOO!!!" I cried when a golden shield rose in front of us. Aiden slammed into me, he was burnt badly. When I touched the burns a golden glow rose from my clawed fingers and spread through his body, healing it.

With my newly released powers I stood in front of Aiden who was obviously in pain but still trying to stop me from fighting the fight that was clearly mine to fight.

"You may disrespect and belittle me since I am new to being a God," I tensed my hand next to my waist turning it to a blade made of light, "but I can't let you hurt my family!" I rushed over to her and began slashing and stabbing at light speed which she tried to dodge and block all the while.

I let out a war cry which purified all of the Shapeless in the room- outside and inside of the Rapture machine. Hope woke up and summoned a bow and arrow of light and shot the machine which pulverized it to nothing but dust of unfixable elements.

Fie realized she was outnumbered and alone, realizing that the human leaders would not listen to her as they were here, watching the fight since the Creator Trio noisily came to the frey. "Screw you mortals, screw you Hope and screw you damned hatchling!" she disappeared in a blaze of glory and I could finally relax. For a little bit at least.

The humans clapped their hands and cheered.

"You aren't mad at us for stopping the machine from activating?" I asked, completely confused, "you worked so hard for this research?"

Scarlet chuckled. "Not at all, my Lady, not at all," she affirmed, "having a program called 'Rapture' didn't sound like a good idea in hindsight, right, you two?"

"Then… you won't ever try this again, right? RIGHT?" I looked at them, almost begging them.

"Yeah…" Kingsone straightened up, "I met with my long lost cousin, who is a leader in her own right now… I should let her live her life now as she desires."

Oliver slammed the strings of his crwth, causing a ruckus. "AS YA SHOULD!" He screeched, "I never thought you really cared that much fer her, though."

So after reconciling in the meeting room once more all leaders agreed to manage their people better and decided to send the most broken soldiers to the town raised by Gods for protection and rehab, and they decided to officially have a ceasefire for at least to the end of all of their terms.

Is this the end?

Up to the humans and the many of existence.

Nightmares still exist.

Corruption has deep roots

And desires never die.

It's all up to your choice after all!

9 781965 732205